# Finally a Bride

## Renee Andrews

⟐ HARLEQUIN® LOVE INSPIRED®

Recycling programs for this product may not exist in your area.

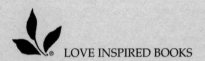 LOVE INSPIRED BOOKS

ISBN-13: 978-1-335-50938-3

Finally a Bride

This edition published by arrangement with Love Inspired Books.

® and TM are trademarks of Love Inspired Books, used under license. Trademarks indicated with ® are registered in the United States Patent and Trademark Office, the Canadian Intellectual Property Office and in other countries.

www.Harlequin.com

**Printed in U.S.A.**

## "I need to get back."

She knew better. He didn't need to get back; he needed to get away.

But she wasn't giving up that easily.

"Today, you were an entirely different person when we drove to the farm, like someone I'd actually like to have as a friend. But then you were downright rude, and for the life of me, I can't figure out why."

If possible, his jaw clenched tighter. Then he closed his eyes and leaned his head back against the seat.

Haley had no idea if he was praying…or counting to ten.

Either way, he'd made her angry.

"Gavin, I'm volunteering my time for this program, and it's going to be a lot of time, from what I can tell. Maybe I should ask if they can get someone else to work with me. If you don't want to…"

"No, I want to do this. And what happened at the barn had nothing to do with you," he growled, his tone filled with heated emotion.

How could she work with this bear of a man?

**Renee Andrews** spends a lot of time in the gym. No, she isn't working out. Her husband, a former All-American gymnast, owns a gym and coaches gymnastics. Renee is a kidney donor and actively supports organ donation. When she isn't writing, she enjoys traveling with her husband and bragging about their sons, daughters-in-law and grandchildren. For more info on her books or on living donors, visit her website at reneeandrews.com.

## Books by Renee Andrews

### Love Inspired

#### *Willow's Haven*

*Family Wanted*
*Second Chance Father*
*Child Wanted*
*Finally a Bride*

*Healing Autumn's Heart*
*Picture Perfect Family*
*Love Reunited*
*Heart of a Rancher*
*Bride Wanted*
*Yuletide Twins*
*Mommy Wanted*
*Small-Town Billionaire*
*Daddy Wanted*

Visit the Author Profile page at Harlequin.com for more titles.

Delight thyself also in the Lord:
and he shall give thee the desires of thine heart.
—*Psalms* 37:4

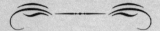

This book is dedicated to
our youngest son, Kaleb Zeringue, and
his beautiful wife, Kaiyla Zeringue. May God
bless each and every day of your life together.

# *Chapter One*

"**I**s he going to *die*?"

The little boy's wailing question echoed down the hallway of Claremont Veterinary Services.

Her first day flying solo as Claremont, Alabama's resident vet, and Haley Calhoun feared she was about to witness a little boy losing his best friend.

Why hadn't Doc Sheridan waited one more day to retire?

She'd pray to God for guidance, but they weren't exactly on speaking terms so she held that thought in check.

"Oh, dear, that doesn't sound good, does it?" Mae Martin petted Snowflake, her finicky Turkish Angora, who was curled up on the exam table. The huge cat's green eyes grew wide, as if she were extremely annoyed by the little boy's cries.

"No, it doesn't." Haley hoped her sole employee, Aaliyah Smith, could assess and handle the situation long enough for her to complete Snowflake's annual checkup. "Mrs. Martin, Snowflake is doing fine, other than the dry-skin issue. Aaliyah has the omega fatty acid supplement I recommended up front if you want to purchase that when you check out." She delivered the statement as quickly as possible, since the cries from the lobby had turned into pitiful, sucking whimpers.

Mae nodded before Haley completed the sentence. "Yes, dear, that's fine." Her silver charm bracelet and heavy bangle jingled as she waved a hand toward the door of the exam room. "You go tend to that baby out front. I'll talk to Aaliyah about those supplements." She reached for Snowflake's pink floral carrier and prepared to coax her contrary pet inside.

"Thanks, Mrs. Martin." Haley moved toward the steel sink in the exam room to wash her hands.

"And I'll be praying for you. I know you're bound to be a little nervous handling things on your own around here with Doc Sheridan moving to Florida, but I can tell you're going to do just fine."

Mrs. Martin had no way of knowing how desperately Haley wanted to do "just fine." She'd always dreamed of having her own veterinary practice, and she'd moved to this tiny Alabama town six years ago specifically because Doc Sheridan had assured her he was on the verge of retirement and ready to turn over his practice to "young blood." But now that he was gone, she felt overwhelmed.

"And the fact that you're starting that new program for the Willow's Haven children to work with animals... well, I admire you greatly for that. Those kids need so much, don't they?"

"Yes, they do." Haley had been so busy getting ready for Doc Sheridan's retirement and learning the details of running the place on her own that she hadn't even visited the children's home yet. But she planned to get the program started this week.

"It's beautiful out there, isn't it, at Willow's Haven?

At least the children have a nice place to live," Mae continued.

Haley washed her hands, dried them and then grabbed three tissues out of the box on the counter. "I haven't actually seen it yet. I've only talked to Brodie and Savvy Evans on the phone." She kept her voice calm as she gathered her courage to face what could be a very bad first day as the only vet in town.

She'd only recently made the decision to help the orphaned and abandoned children cope with their losses by giving them animals to care for, but listening to the cries in her lobby made her wonder if it might not always be a positive experience.

"Oh, you're in for a treat. Willow's Haven is beautiful, and so peaceful. The church put an announcement about the upcoming program in our bulletin last week. By the way, we've missed you there, dear," Mae called out, bringing up yet another uncomfortable topic while Haley strode down the hall toward the lobby.

"Thanks," she answered, not making any promises about seeing her there any time soon. Instead she made a beeline toward the wailing boy.

"I found him—" his watery hazel eyes focused on Aaliyah, who was leaning down to look at the teeny ball of fur cradled in his arms "—in the woods behind our cabin. I think he's scared. I thought he was hungry, but he wouldn't eat my snack. And Mr. Gavin said I shouldn't try to feed him anything else until he sees the doctor."

Haley noted that the boy was wearing a puffy blue winter coat and red mittens, even though it was merely late October. A light dusting of dirt coated his face, barring the tear streaks striping both full cheeks. More dirt was missing beneath his nose, which dripped from crying. He looked around six or seven years old, best Haley could tell, but with worry lines as intense as her grandfather's currently creasing his forehead.

She should have grabbed more tissues.

Wasting no time in crouching to his eye level, she performed a perfunctory scan of the quivering puppy in his arms. A mixed breed, brown and black, with quite a bit of Yorkie in him. Bones were visible beneath his thin coat but, at first glance, none appeared to be broken. Probably dropped off on the side of the road, poor thing.

"He wouldn't eat my snack. I tried to feed him, but he wouldn't eat it."

Haley took one of the tissues and tenderly wiped beneath the boy's left eye, then followed suit with the right. Doubling up the last two tissues, she asked, "Can you blow your nose for me?"

He nodded, placed his nose in the center and proceeded to make a sound like something she'd expect to hear from one of her animals instead of a darling little boy. Sniffing, he completed by rubbing his nose against the tissues before glancing at Haley. "Sorry. I blow loud."

She smiled. "Yes, you do, but that's okay." She wiped the wadded tissues beneath his nose again, then tossed them in a small trash can in the lobby. "What's your name?"

Another sniff. "Eli."

"That's a nice name."

"It's from the Bible." His eyes blinked overtime to battle more tears.

Haley nodded, not wanting to stir the pot by acknowledging she knew the story about Eli and Samuel. Mrs. Martin would enter the lobby soon, and Haley didn't want any additional reminders that she should be at church. Therefore, she changed her focus from the boy's name to the quivering animal and held her palm in front of the puppy's nose. He made no attempt to move toward her to get a better scent, which should have come from mere instinct. "And what is this little guy's name?"

"Mr. Gavin called him Buddy when we found him in the woods."

Haley glanced toward the opposite side of the lobby, where a man had his back turned to her and talked quietly on his phone. Mr. Gavin, she presumed. He didn't seem overly concerned with the little boy's dilemma, which didn't earn him any brownie points in Haley's book. Was he the boy's stepdad? A teacher? Mom's apathetic boyfriend?

It bothered her tremendously to see adults neglecting a child. Her own parents had been amazing at supporting her growing up, attending every activity and encouraging her through every step of her veterinary dreams.

A shame that, after being the model husband to her mother and perfect dad to Haley, her father had turned his back on them completely.

She winced, not wanting to go *there* again.

The truth was, in spite of her dad eventually letting her down, she'd wanted to be the kind of parent and have the kind of family she'd had growing up. She'd wanted children desperately and had planned to have at least one by the time she was thirty.

That milestone birthday had passed last month and since she'd now decided against all dating and relationships, children certainly weren't in the picture. But she could still be around and show them that someone cared. That'd been her main reason for wanting to start the new Adopt-an-Animal program for Willow's Haven.

Mr. Gavin continued talking on his phone and Haley all but snarled toward his back.

She returned her attention to the one who needed it. "Buddy—that's a great name." She scanned the puppy. His fur was dull and brittle, eyes opened marginally then closed again, as if he didn't have the energy to look at who held him. Running a finger along his back, she easily felt his spine, which would have been visible had it not been for a thin layer of scruffy, dry hair.

"He wouldn't eat my fruit snacks," Eli said, anxious to provide insight as to what was wrong with his new friend. He'd made this statement a couple of times already, obviously wanting her to know he'd done his best to assist the little pup.

Haley nodded. "He hasn't eaten a lot of food in a while, so he'll have to take his time learning to eat normally again. But it was very thoughtful of you to try to feed him."

Eli's top teeth tugged his lower lip, his eyes blinking as he soaked up every word.

"Think about when you're sick. When you aren't feeling well, do you eat a lot?"

"Just soup. And maybe Sprite." He was absolutely adorable, with his dirty little face and pleading eyes, and so concerned for the puppy in his arms.

"Right. Well, he will need to work up to eating again, too, like you do after you've been sick." She'd continued probing and performing a preexam on the tiny dog while talking to the boy, and she was now fairly certain that no bones were broken. The pup didn't show signs of distemper, and though his breathing was shallow, he wasn't struggling for breath. Even so, he wasn't out of the woods yet. She would need to keep him for treatment, and she hoped the boy would understand.

"He doesn't eat soup, does he?" Eli asked. "'Cause I could get him some if that'll make him better."

"No, he doesn't, but I can try some other things that his tummy should be okay with, until he can work his way up to eating normal food again." She placed a finger under Eli's chin. "Would that be okay, for me to take care of him here for a little while? To help him feel better?" Haley knew the puppy wouldn't have made it very long in the woods on his own. This little boy, whether he realized it or not, had potentially saved him.

"Do I *have* to leave him here?" The panic in his voice pierced her heart and his grip on the puppy increased, so that the little animal let out a squeaky yelp.

Haley barely noticed the man on the other side of the lobby turn to face them, because she was too intent on capturing the boy's attention. "Eli, calm down, honey. I am going to do my best to get him well. I promise."

He stared at the puppy, still whimpering. "Did I *hurt* him?"

"You just don't need to squeeze him so much," she said. "But I can tell that you aren't trying to hurt him, and he knows that, too."

"He does?" Eli looked imploringly to Haley. "Are you sure?"

She nodded. "Of course. Puppies can tell when someone cares about them, just like people can tell when someone cares about them." She fought the impulse to glare at the man who had shifted his stance and was now undoubtedly watching their interaction.

"I want to keep him." Eli took a small step away from Haley. "He doesn't have anyone to love him, and he's scared."

A muffled clearing of a throat caused Haley to finally glance up at Mr. Gavin and, for a moment, her breath caught in her chest. Not what she'd expected. She'd anticipated an older, grumpy, stern-faced gentleman who wouldn't show concern for the brokenhearted boy. But this man was young, around Haley's age, she'd guess, with one of the most strikingly masculine faces she'd ever seen.

Haley swallowed, forcing herself to get a grip on the awareness flooding through her. She wouldn't be swayed by his gorgeous good looks and rugged presence.

The bottom line was that he didn't seem to care about this little boy's pain.

And that was reason enough for Haley to dislike the man.

So when he glared at Haley, she glared right back.

Gavin Thomason had thought taking the seven-year-olds from his cabin for an adventure hike would be a great way to enjoy the crisp October afternoon.

The Claremont Community Church had bought the kids new coats, hats and gloves this afternoon for the upcoming winter months. Knowing the boys had been eager to try out their new things, he'd thought the hike had seemed like a great idea.

So, after assisting all of them with their homework, he'd given each boy a sheet with photos of leaves to find and told them they could don their new winter duds for the adventure, even though the temperature was in the midsixties. He'd planned to talk to them about the different trees God created, about the leaves changing color and about how God gave us seasonal weather to enjoy throughout the year. He'd anticipated this leading into the afternoon devotional, focusing on how, in God's world, things change. And, more importantly, on how change didn't always mean something bad.

Since all the kids at the children's home had gone through tremendous life changes, he'd thought the devotional would be well received. That it would help them deal with their unique circumstances, whether they'd been orphaned, abandoned or neglected by their families.

But once Eli had heard that puppy's cry, all Gavin's plans for the afternoon had flown out the window.

Mark Laverty, one of Gavin's fellow cabin counselors, had taken over today's activity so Gavin could take Eli and what appeared to be a dying puppy to the vet. Gavin had prayed the whole way here because, of all the boys in his cabin, none had been through as much pain as Eli. And none had touched Gavin's heart like he had, because he'd lost everything that had mattered in his world…

Just like Gavin.

"Do I have to *leave* him here?" Eli turned away from the vet to direct the question to his cabin counselor. "I don't want to leave him, Mr. Gavin. He's scared."

The vet, whom Gavin had barely acknowledged until this point, glanced up from where she crouched next to the boy. Gavin focused on the woman who, at this moment, could hurt the child more than anyone else if she didn't help this pitiful dog. And he wasn't all that certain of her ability to do so. She certainly didn't look like any vet he'd ever seen before. She was young, probably a little younger than Gavin's thirty-one, with vivid green eyes amid a pixie face, pale pink gloss on heart-shaped lips and long blond hair that hung well past her shoulders.

How hadn't he noticed her before now? And why had he picked today, of all days, to become even remotely aware of an attractive female?

Regardless, he wasn't ready, or willing, to let his mind start noticing such things as green eyes, glossy lips or silky hair.

Not yet. Maybe not ever.

*God, help me.*

"Buddy needs to stay here, if you want him to have the best chance…" Her voice drifted off, but Gavin knew where the statement had been headed.

*…for survival.*

Then his mind honed in on the fact that she'd called the dog by name.

"Buddy?" he asked. Was she familiar with the pup? Did she know the owner? Or whoever had abandoned him?

Eli sniffed. "That's his name. That's what you called him when we found him."

Well, what do you know? Gavin had unintentionally named the pup. He'd merely told the little tuft of fur, whining in a pile of leaves and pine straw, *We'll take care of you, buddy.*

And now, thanks to Gavin, they had a "Buddy," and one that Eli didn't want to leave behind.

He did his best not to notice that the vet was even lovelier when she looked at the puppy and boy with such compassion. Steeling his heart for her answer, he asked her directly, "Are you *able* to heal him?" He didn't want to get Eli's hopes up if she knew the tiny dog's chances were slim to nil.

Her cheeks twitched slightly, eyes narrowing the slightest bit.

Gavin noticed.

But he didn't care.

He wanted an honest answer about the dog's chances, because he wouldn't lie to Eli, not about this puppy or anything else. The little guy already had enough tough blows to last a lifetime, and Gavin wouldn't allow this young doctor to cause him more unnecessary pain.

She looked away from Gavin, her features softening as she placed a hand beneath the puppy's scruffy chin. "He's severely malnourished, and it'll take time to get him back to a healthy condition. He's undoubtedly been on his own for a few days." She looked like she wanted to explain further, but Eli emitted another sucking whimper that made her pause and drape an arm around him.

"But, yes, I do know what to do to try and make him better." The last sentence was delivered to the little boy beside her rather than the man who had asked the question.

Gavin prayed that the woman who sounded so convincing…hadn't just lied to the kid.

"But I have to *leave* him here?" Eli repeated, this time his lip quivering through the words.

"So I can take extra good care of him." She tenderly brushed a tear from his cheek. "Is that okay, Eli?"

"But what if—what if he *dies*? What if he goes to Heaven, too?" He looked toward Gavin and then back at the doctor. "What if I was too late—again? Like I was too late when Mommy and Daddy died?"

Gavin felt punched in the gut. Last year, the kid, at only six years old, had tried earnestly to save his parents, even after all the adults around him had given up.

The vet bit down on her lower lip and Gavin could tell that she was trying to control the emotions pressing forward at the hint of Eli's tragic past. And he recognized the same deep sorrow that he felt every time he thought of the way this little boy had been left, all alone, with no one to care for him.

Much like that little dog in the woods.

"I'm going to do my very best to make sure that doesn't happen," she promised.

"Can I come see him, though? Like, every day?" Eli shifted the quivering dog to one arm and wiped the opposite red mitten across his cheek to knock the tears away before returning it to cradle the pup. "Can I come after school? He needs to know that I love him. It's important. I'll need to show him."

She blinked twice, held on to that lower lip a long beat before finally speaking. "That would be very nice, and I know it would comfort him to know you care."

Eli nuzzled the puppy, who had fallen asleep in his arms. "Can I, Mr. Gavin? Can I come see him every day until he's better?"

"Yes," he said gruffly, as if any other answer would escape his lips. "I'll bring you after school, after you finish your homework. But you need to give the puppy—Buddy—to Dr..." He'd noticed her name embroidered on her white jacket, but from this angle, he couldn't read the script.

"Calhoun," she supplied, and then she softened that clear, lyrical voice, looked at Eli and said, "or you can call me Miss Haley."

Haley Calhoun. The name sparked a hint of a memory, something he'd overheard recently, but he couldn't recall what was said.

Gavin shook the scattered thought away and nodded to Eli. "Now give Buddy to Dr. Calhoun, so she can take care of him and help him get better."

Eli eased the lifeless animal toward the doctor. "O-kay."

Her eyebrows dropped, fingers probing gently as she took the puppy.

Trying to divert the boy's attention from the doctor's sudden look of concern, Gavin pointed to the school-bag Eli had dropped near a chair by the door. "Eli, why don't you grab your backpack and get ready to go? We'll come see Buddy again tomorrow."

Gavin's phone rang and he saw that Savvy Evans, who ran the children's home with her husband, Brodie, was on the other end. No doubt she wanted an update on the mistreated puppy. He answered, "Hey Savvy, we're still at the vet."

Eli halted his pace toward the backpack. "Can I tell Miss Savvy about Buddy?"

Gavin nodded. "Savvy, Eli wants to talk to you." He gave him the phone and listened as the boy recited every detail, from holding the puppy on the way to the vet to everything Haley—Dr. Calhoun—had said since they'd arrived.

While Eli was occupied talking, Gavin took the opportunity to approach the doctor, now quietly instructing her assistant about Buddy's initial course of treatment. The assistant left for a moment and then returned with a blue blanket in her arms.

"It's warm?" Haley asked, and the other woman, who looked around twenty, nodded. Then the doctor tenderly transferred the pup, as though he were extremely fragile, to the blanket in the assistant's arms.

"Hello, Mr. Thomason," the younger blonde said.

Gavin was clueless and apparently showed it.

"Aaliyah Smith. I go to church with you," she offered, "at Claremont Community Church."

"Right." He hated the fact that he was so often preoccupied with his own world that he rarely noticed others, even during religious services. Or maybe, he was so often preoccupied with his past that he rarely noticed the present.

But he noticed the children in his care, and most everyone else who was involved with helping the boys in his cabin.

Aaliyah gave him a soft smile, presumably not offended that he hadn't recognized her, and then hurried to the back with the dog. Observing her haste, Gavin feared the worst. So while Eli continued telling Savvy about Buddy, he moved toward the doctor and touched her shoulder. "You *can't* let that puppy die."

Unfortunately his words came out brusquely, more like a command than a request.

The vet's eyes widened, her mouth formed a small O and then she stole a glance at Eli, still talking, before lowering her voice to match his. "I can promise you I will do my best to bring him back to good health. That's my job, and I take my job very seriously."

Gavin wasn't influenced by the fact that he'd irritated her. He needed answers, pure and simple.

"Okay, what does that involve? What's wrong with the dog, and what are you planning to do?" He hated the accusatory tone, but he also couldn't control it. Whether she liked it or not, she'd become a key factor in whether Eli lost something else he cared about, and Gavin wasn't about to let that happen. Not on his watch.

She narrowed those green eyes again. He'd offended her. That hadn't been his intention, but if it got him the information he needed, so be it.

"Buddy has been on his own for at least three or four days. He is dehydrated and needs to be treated for parasites." Her voice had taken on a clinical tone that he knew all too well. It'd been the same one the doctor had used when Gavin received the news that his wife—the true love of his life—died giving birth to their son. And then, merely an hour later…that their baby boy had died, too.

Two years ago today.

Gritting his teeth to combat the pain of the past, he forced himself to listen while the doctor continued.

"We will start by putting him in a quiet, safe area away from other animals, lights and activity. We want to keep him as calm as possible. Aaliyah is taking his temperature now, but he felt cool, so we've wrapped him in a warm blanket and will regulate his temperature slowly. If this is done too quickly, it could harm his delicate nervous system."

Gavin kept an eye on Eli while he took advantage of his preoccupation to learn more about what the doctor planned for Buddy's treatment. "And then what?"

Still in that clinical tone he loathed, she explained in detail the steps planned to help the pup.

She paused when a white-haired woman carrying a pink floral bag walked toward the lobby from one of the exam rooms. The bag mewed continually as she crossed the floor. White fur and green eyes pushed against the mesh end.

"Why, Mr. Thomason, what brings you here?" Mae Martin asked. Then she saw Eli, his back facing her as he talked on the phone on the other side of the lobby. "Oh, my, was that crying child I heard one of your darling boys?"

"Yes, ma'am."

Mae was a regular visitor to Willow's Haven, one of the volunteers who read library books to the children. The readers had become a part of the kids' world, so that, even though they didn't have a real family, they still had a family of sorts through Willow's Haven and the small Claremont community. Mae had been assigned to Gavin's cabin, so she knew each child. Her eyes moved to Eli, who'd turned in her direction but was still too focused on his conversation to notice Mae.

She shook her head. "Bless his little heart. Those children have already been through so much. I could tell he was upset when I heard him crying, but I didn't realize when I was in the back that it was Eli. Such a tender-hearted child. Is everything going to be okay?"

"It will be." He looked pointedly to the doctor. "Right?"

"That's. My. Goal," she said, her words clipped.

"Well, you won't find a better vet than our Haley, that's for sure," Mae said. "She and Doc Sheridan have been taking care of Snowflake for five years now." She pointed a finger at the vet. "And, like I told you, don't you worry about being on your own now that he's retired. You're going to do a great job here." She smiled at Gavin. "Today's her first day on her own, you know."

Not what Gavin wanted to hear. His face must've shown it because those green eyes grew sharper, daring him to comment. He held his words.

"Thank you, Mrs. Martin," Haley said as Aaliyah returned to the front counter.

Gavin knew better than to say anything else to the doctor about his fears, so he turned to Aaliyah. "The puppy—he's doing okay?"

"He is," she answered with a smile. "Temperature is coming up. I have him under the warmer while he's waiting to be seen by Dr. Calhoun."

"Great." Gavin nodded once toward her then returned his focus to the veterinarian while Aaliyah spoke to Mrs. Martin. "How long do you expect the treatment to take?"

Again, looking incredulously at him but answering calmly, she explained, "There is no way to know, but the minimum amount of time I'd anticipate to stabilize him is around seventy-two hours. That wouldn't be when he's ready to be released, but stable enough to begin eating and hydrating normally." Glancing toward Eli, she added softly, "He could be here awhile."

Gavin couldn't control his frown. Eli wouldn't be happy about that, but if it was necessary, then that's what would have to happen. "As long as you keep him alive and get him better, that's fine."

One eyebrow lifted slightly. "I'm so glad that's fine for you."

Gavin hadn't been much of a people person over the past couple of years. He had a big heart for children and had always interacted with them well, but the ability to communicate effectively with adults, particularly attractive females, no longer fell into his list of finer attributes. Clearly that was still the case with this vet.

Which was fine. He didn't want anything beyond a surface acquaintance with any woman. "We'll stop by tomorrow then, after school, so Eli can see for himself that Buddy is getting better." Then, without giving her a chance to respond, he turned to the boy clicking the end button on the cell. "Come on, Eli. We'll come back tomorrow."

"Okay, Mr. Gavin," he said, handing him the phone. Then he rushed into the arms of Haley Calhoun. "And please get him well for me, Miss Haley. Okay?"

Gavin waited for her to give the correct response.

"I will do my best."

The little boy who held Gavin's heart in his hands

turned and gave him the first semblance of a smile since finding the puppy. He truly believed the vet could save Buddy.

Gavin forced a smile and prayed for God to heal the pup, because he didn't want to be there if Eli's heart was shattered again. He had a feeling it would take God's intervention, too, for the animal to pull through.

Mae Martin turned from the counter toward Eli. "Why, Miss Haley will take the absolute best care of your little Buddy."

The memory Gavin had sensed earlier clicked into place and he recalled exiting the cabin to find Mrs. Martin speaking to Savvy about her concern for a former church member. Haley Calhoun.

*What a shame*, she'd said, *that such a beautiful young lady who'd been so involved in the congregation seems to have given up on God when she gave up on men.*

## Chapter Two

Even though her office would close in five minutes, Haley still sat at the computer behind the front counter entering notes from her last patient.

She couldn't focus. Instead of thinking about the details pertaining to Abi Cutter's accident-prone chocolate Lab, Roscoe, who'd pried the lid off a bin of horse feed and eaten more than his share, she continued dwelling on her earlier interaction with Gavin Thomason.

She hadn't missed the fact that he'd been talking to Savvy Evans, who ran Willow's Haven with her husband. That, coupled with Eli's statement that his parents were in Heaven, told her this little boy would be one of the children she could help with her new program.

Did it also mean she'd be dealing with Mr. Gavin, too?

She cringed at the thought.

"Roscoe seems to be doing better now," Aaliyah told her, returning from checking on their "overnighters." Today they had four animals currently in their long-term care: Buddy; two golden retrievers, Honey and Sugar, currently boarded while their owners were on vacation in Tennessee; and Roscoe.

"I'm glad to hear that." Haley clicked a few keys on the computer. "We probably would've been fine letting Roscoe go home with the Cutters, but I'd like to watch him overnight." She was also glad Aaliyah's presence helped her to focus on the task at hand—documenting their most frequent customer—instead of dwelling on the man who had gotten under her skin like a burr beneath a saddle blanket.

"Honestly, Roscoe probably sees this place as his home away from home." Aaliyah smirked. "Isn't this his third time in the past month?"

Haley scrolled through Roscoe's file. "Fourth, if you count when I treated him on-site."

"Oh, yeah, when he got his head stuck in that fence rail. I forgot all about that." Aaliyah sprayed the counter with disinfectant and began wiping it down. "You should start using the bigger office now that Doc Sheridan is gone."

"I'm comfortable here." Haley liked being visible to clients as much as possible. Plus, Aaliyah only worked two days per week so, most of the time, Haley would be the only one to greet customers, maintain files and treat patients. Before, she'd had Doc Sheridan to share in that burden. But she didn't mind staying busy. Beyond talking to her mother and grandfather on an almost-daily basis, the animals provided her primary semblance of family now.

And she was okay with that. Really.

She completed the notes on Roscoe and closed his file, which brought Buddy's to the forefront of her computer. "How did Buddy handle that bit of liquids?"

"Kept everything down so far. He's sleeping again."

"Poor little thing." He'd been covered in almost as much dirt as Eli when he'd arrived and was just as cute.

She looked forward to seeing the boy again tomorrow when he came to visit the puppy and anticipated Buddy might be a little more responsive after twenty-four hours of hydration.

The alarm went off on Aaliyah's cell. "Closing time. Ready to call it a day?" She lifted her brow. "Until you come back to check on the animals before bed, that is. Why don't you come to the ladies' Bible study tonight at Mandy Brantley's house? You seemed to enjoy it that one time you came."

"Did I?" Haley kept her eyes on the computer screen while silently willing her assistant to drop the subject. But after waiting a couple of beats, she glanced up to see Aaliyah's frown.

"Okay, so you didn't. But we enjoyed having you there. Have you had a chance to look at the new study we're doing on forgiveness?" She tapped the thin blue book she'd given Haley last week, still sitting on the desk where Haley had put it that day.

"No, not yet. And I think I'll pass, but thanks for the invitation." She saved Buddy's file and shut down the computer.

Before Aaliyah could plead her case further, like she did each week, the office door burst open. Mae Martin entered, bracelets jangling as she waved off her apologies.

"I'm so sorry, Haley. I know you're about to close up shop for the day, but I realized after I started getting Snowflake's dinner ready that I left those supplements here. I'm beginning to believe I'd lose my head if it weren't attached." She laughed and crossed the lobby to where Aaliyah had already reached beneath the counter and pulled out the white bottle.

"You must have placed them behind the computer

when you were writing your check," Aaliyah said. "I found them after you left." She placed the bottle in a brown paper bag this time, probably so Mrs. Martin would have a better chance of keeping up with it.

Mae leaned over the counter toward Haley. "Tell me, how's that little puppy doing? I could tell Gavin was concerned about him."

"He's doing better," Haley said, frustrated that Gavin's lack of confidence had been so easily visible.

"Good. That little boy has been through so much already." She looked knowingly toward Haley. "I'm sure that's why Gavin was intent on making sure the little pup would be okay."

"He isn't always so full of sunshine?" Haley didn't disguise her sarcasm.

Mae put a hand to her chest, laughing deeply. "Oh, my, you've got his number already, don't you? Actually he's always like that around adults. But when you see him around those kids at Willow's Haven, especially Eli, you get a glimpse of the heart hiding beneath the surface. Both Brodie and Savvy will tell you that he's one of the best cabin counselors they have." She tilted her head and lifted one corner of her mouth in a smile. "Gavin's a good guy. He's just a pro at hiding it."

Haley wondered why that was. And why, if he was so good with kids, he didn't have an equal affinity toward adults.

Then she shook those questions away. She didn't need to be wondering anything about the devastatingly handsome and undeniably annoying man. Plus, they were already fifteen minutes past closing and she had no desire to prolong this discussion.

Mae started toward the door, then stopped and pointed beneath one of the lobby chairs. "Oh, dear.

That's Eli's backpack. I'm sure he'll need it for school tomorrow. I hope he isn't upset at leaving it. He's already had such a bad day, being worried about the puppy and all." She turned and frowned. "I'd take it to him, but I need to get back and feed Snowflake."

"And I need to get home to see Cierrah," Aaliyah said, referring to her adorable four-year-old daughter.

Mae's smile widened. "Looks like you'll probably need to take this out to the children's home, hmm? You wouldn't want Eli to be sad about leaving it, and you'll definitely want to make sure he has it for school tomorrow."

Haley stared at the red-and-blue backpack then stole a glance at the two women, smiling and nodding at each other as though thrilled with this predicament. "If I didn't know any better, I'd say one of you left it there so I'd have to go see that bear of a man."

"You *are* good with animals." Aaliyah barely stifled her giggle.

Mae winked at her, charm bracelet clanging as she pointed a pink-tipped finger her way. "Oh, that was good."

Haley did her best to ignore any additional remarks, because both ladies were obviously on a roll.

With a heavy sigh, she headed for the door.

"Eli is really taken with that dog, isn't he?" Mark asked while he and Gavin rode in the front seats of the Willow's Haven bus with some of the other cabin counselors. Most of the kids behind them chattered about this evening's soccer practice. But Eli, who sat a couple of rows back and had a voice a little louder than the average seven-year-old, couldn't stop talking about Buddy.

Gavin glanced over his shoulder at the boy. "Yeah, he is."

"So, does the vet think the dog will be okay with treatment? Because I'm not sure how Eli will take it if he isn't."

Gavin wasn't surprised the other man's thoughts mirrored his own. "She said she would do her best."

"She? You didn't take him to Doc Sheridan?"

"From what I gather, he retired, and this was the new vet's first day on the job."

"Aw, man, that doesn't sound good for Eli's puppy." Mark propped his arm on the back of the seat and ran his hand across his mouth in a that's-too-bad move.

Gavin felt the same way. "Yeah. Well, according to Mrs. Martin, she's been there for a while working as his assistant, so I'm praying she'll be able to help."

"Wait a minute. Doc Sheridan's assistant? Haley? Haley Calhoun?" Mark asked, his tone livening with every syllable. "*She's* the vet taking care of the puppy?"

"Yeah. Why?"

"I didn't realize you were talking about Haley. She's awesome. I'm surprised you haven't seen her around town already. She'll be coming to Willow's Haven on a regular basis soon, since she's the one running the new Adopt-an-Animal program, where she'll bring animals to Willow's Haven." He smiled broadly. "We'll also be taking the kids out to the Cutter Ranch to spend time with the horses, hiking and all of that, and I'm sure she'll be part of that, as well. It was Haley's idea, actually, and she's donating her time. Pretty cool."

Gavin wasn't certain how "cool" it'd be. He hadn't liked that niggling attraction he'd felt when he'd seen the pretty lady, and he certainly didn't want to experience it on a regular basis. Especially when he had no desire for any relationship again. He'd had the perfect relationship, with Selah, and he didn't want—or need—another.

Maybe he wouldn't have to see the good doctor when she worked with the kids.

Yeah, right. His cabin would undoubtedly be involved with the Adopt-an-Animal program, so he'd be interacting, in some manner, with Haley Calhoun. Even after they finished seeing each other because of Eli's puppy.

Gavin swallowed past the grumble in his throat.

Thankfully, Mark didn't seem to notice. "She'll do her best with the puppy," he said, nodding, "I feel certain of that."

And that's what she'd told Gavin. That she'd do her best. He just hadn't trusted her best to be good enough. Selah's doctors had also said they would do their best. But Mark sure seemed to trust Dr. Haley Calhoun. "How do you know her?"

Mark shifted in his seat, scanned the group of boys behind them and answered, "When I first moved to Claremont, I had an English-American bulldog mix named Roman. When I took Roman to the vet, I'd typically see Haley. She did a great job. Roman was old already, lived a couple of years past his life expectancy, and Haley was so gentle with him. That dog loved her." He shrugged. "I don't see her that often anymore. Used to see her at the church, but she hasn't been there in a while."

Gavin recalled Mae's comment that Haley'd given up on God when she'd given up on men and he wondered what had happened in the feisty vet's world. He knew personally what it was like to give up on God. He'd given up on Him, gotten angry at Him, on this very day two years ago. But then, he'd felt so alone and eventually recognized that the One he blamed…was the only One who could heal his pain.

While Gavin contemplated what had happened to the lovely vet, Eli's voice overpowered the others on the crowded bus. "And then Miss Haley told me that I could come and see him every day after school," he told Ryan, the boy sitting beside him.

"I wish *I* could find a puppy in the woods," Ryan said.

Mark grinned. "Some things never change. Every little boy wants a dog."

Brodie Evans, sitting on the opposite bench seat, nodded. "Savvy and I were actually discussing that this afternoon. Dylan, Rose and Daisy have been asking for a dog and we think the new Adopt-an-Animal program might be good for all the children."

"I can see how that could benefit the kids," Gavin agreed, even if he wasn't thrilled about the vet who would lead the program. She made him uncomfortable, set him off balance. However, he remembered how protective Eli had been of the puppy this afternoon. And how much he hadn't wanted to leave him behind.

"We just want to make sure we can keep animals on site before we get them for our kids, because we wouldn't want Dylan, Rose and Daisy to have pets if all of the other children couldn't have animals, too."

Brodie and Savvy were amazing at not only taking care of the needs of their own children but also those of the children in their care. In fact, after learning about the Christian environment and the way they provided for children, Gavin had moved from Memphis just to work at Willow's Haven. He'd also considered an amazing children's home in Oregon, but had decided that, while he wanted to get away from the town where he'd made a home with Selah, he hadn't wanted to move clear across the country.

Mark leaned forward in his seat. "So we'd have to get it approved by the state before Eli could keep the pup?"

"Yeah, we need to cover our bases and make sure everything is okay before making any changes at the home," Brodie said. "But Savvy is planning to give the social worker a call tomorrow and ask. I think the only hesitation is that the kids might bond with the animals and then, when they are placed in a permanent home, won't want to leave them behind."

"Maybe some of the adoptive parents would consider adopting a pet, too," Mark said, grinning. "Sounds like a win-win to me."

"That's exactly what Savvy said." Brodie tilted his head toward Gavin. "Eli could barely concentrate on kicking the soccer ball tonight because he kept wanting to tell the other kids about Buddy."

Gavin, who had been attempting to coach Eli's team, nodded. "Trust me, I noticed. He was so busy talking, he almost got pegged with the ball a couple of times."

Brodie chuckled. "Well, maybe when Buddy is better and Eli gets more time with the dog, he'll pay more attention at practice."

"That's assuming we get the okay to keep the dog at Willow's Haven." Gavin decided he would add that to his current prayer requests. Not only for Buddy to get better for Eli's sake, but also that the boy would be allowed to keep the dog he cared so much about.

Mark laughed as Eli's voice took on even more volume. "It's good to see him excited about something, though, isn't it?" he asked.

"Sure is." In fact, Gavin was very glad for that. Seeing a kid who'd been through so much pain find hope again, even if it was directed toward a near-dying dog, gave him encouragement for himself. That maybe one day he wouldn't feel that deep void inside. The one that had only grown since he'd walked out of that hospital—alone—two years ago, a diaper bag he no longer needed draped on one arm and Selah's overnight bag, filled with clothes and items she'd never use again, on the other.

He thought of the blue blouse she'd planned to wear when they left the hospital. And the tiny matching blue coming-home outfit they'd purchased for their baby boy to wear when she carried him in her arms.

Gavin pinched the bridge of his nose and begged God to control the memories and get him through the remainder of this day...some way, somehow.

"Hey, there's Miss Haley! Maybe she brought Buddy!" Eli bellowed.

Gavin moved his hand from his face, took a deep breath and turned to see Willow's Haven cabins come into view and the object of Eli's excitement.

His chest constricted as his gaze rested on the pretty vet standing beside Savvy on Brodie and Savvy's front porch, bright rays of the setting sun highlighting her white-blond hair. Even though she shielded her eyes from the light, Gavin knew that, if he could see them now, they'd shimmer the most vivid emerald green.

He'd thought of those eyes, the hair, the striking features of the woman, a couple of times—or more—since they'd left her office this afternoon. And hated that he hadn't been able to completely get her off his mind.

That wasn't like him.

And he didn't like feeling this way.

Especially not today.

## Chapter Three

"Here comes the bus now." Savvy pointed toward the archway of trees that formed the lengthy driveway to the children's home.

Haley shielded her eyes from the setting sun to spot the bright yellow bus coming into view. Her stomach fluttered. Not so much because of how anxious she was to make sure Eli received his schoolbag, but because seeing the boy would undoubtedly equate to also seeing the formidable man that'd brought him and Buddy to her office earlier.

She'd chatted with Savvy while waiting for the kids to return from soccer practice instead of merely leaving the backpack, partly because she'd wanted to fine-tune the details on the Adopt-an-Animal program and partly because she hadn't stopped thinking about Eli and wanted to let him know how Buddy was doing. But now she second-guessed her decision to hang around. If she'd simply left the backpack, she'd have lessened the chance of seeing the grumpy man again.

Then again, maybe Gavin Thomason wasn't on that bus.

"So who went with the kids to soccer practice? Like,

which adults?" She tried not to make it sound as though she was referring to anyone in particular.

Savvy wasn't fooled. "Gavin *is* on the bus." She leaned one hip against the porch rail. "I'm guessing he wasn't on his best behavior at your office today?"

"You mean he has a best behavior?" Haley, still shielding her eyes, turned away from the approaching bus to face her new friend. She had developed a huge respect and appreciation for Savvy over the past few weeks while they'd discussed the program over the phone and via emails. Even more so after seeing Willow's Haven firsthand.

Mae Martin hadn't lied. The circle of cabins nestled in the center of the woods was beautiful. Peaceful. And with the colorful fall foliage creating a kaleidoscope of reds, oranges and golds in the surrounding woods, the location felt extremely welcoming. Warm and inviting.

She was glad Doc Sheridan had encouraged her to use her experience to benefit the community and to let the town of Claremont truly get to know the newest veterinarian. He'd been the one who'd thought she should find a way to help the children at Willow's Haven. However, he obviously hadn't realized that one of the counselors she'd be working with would be such a ray of sunshine.

"Bless your heart." Savvy moved one finger to her mouth in an effort to cover her smile. "But things aren't always as they seem. Gavin has been through an awful lot in his past, and he really felt God leading him to work with the kids here. He's one of our best counselors, even if he isn't so much of a people person when it comes to adults sometimes."

"And I managed to get on his bad side from the get-go? Just because I couldn't guarantee that I could heal the puppy? I told him I would do my best, and I intend to, but to make that kind of promise…"

Savvy sighed heavily. "Bless his heart. He doesn't want Eli to lose that puppy."

"I don't, either. Like I told him, I'm going to do everything I can to heal him, but I don't see why he had to insinuate that I wasn't capable." Especially her first day on her own. She'd been nervous enough, but to add a customer who had no faith whatsoever in her abilities didn't do anything for her confidence.

The brakes on the bus squeaked loudly as it eased to a stop at the far end of the cabins.

"They will be here soon, but you should know that any other day, Gavin might not have come across quite so grizzly." Savvy frowned, looked as if she debated what else to say before adding, "Brodie thinks he's got a tough personality. *I* think he's merely protecting himself from getting too close to anyone again. But that's me guessing. Only God knows for sure."

"Protecting himself?" Why would he feel the need to shield himself from her?

"As I mentioned, he's been through a lot, but having him here *is* a blessing for these kids. Particularly for Eli."

Haley wondered what the man had been through to make him such a grouch and why her friend thought he was such a blessing for Eli, but Savvy didn't elaborate.

"You'll get a chance to see the good in Gavin, I'm sure, with the Adopt-an-Animal program. Brodie and I have decided he'd be great as your main point of contact at Willow's Haven for the new program."

"What did *he* have to say about that?"

"We plan to tell him in the morning."

Haley winced. After their first meeting she didn't imagine that would go over well at all.

A waving Brodie Evans caused them to look toward the bus. He wore a red T-shirt that matched those of the kids around him, scrambling eagerly as they exited the bus.

Savvy returned the wave with a grin. "Eli should be getting off soon."

"That's great," Haley said, even if she knew that meant the bear would also arrive soon.

A group of boys in green T-shirts climbed off next, with a man in the center. No sign of Eli or Gavin.

Yet.

"Soccer went well," Brodie said to his wife as he neared the porch. "A little better once we convinced them it wasn't cold enough for their winter coats."

Savvy laughed and then explained to Haley. "The church gave the boys their new winter clothing today. Most of them aren't used to getting new things, so they wanted to wear it all immediately."

Haley smiled. "Eli had on a jacket and mittens earlier. I thought it was a little much for the temperature outside, but I didn't say anything."

Brodie laughed. "Yeah, he was the last one to admit he was hot, but he ended up taking it off for practice."

"So, how did the teams do?" Savvy asked.

"I don't expect we'll win a lot of games, but we'll do okay. The guys are having fun."

"That's what matters." She gave a reassuring smile to Haley and then also to her husband. "I'm not so sure the Willow's Haven girls will win any games, either, but they had a good time at their practice last night. Rose and Daisy were excited about their new pink T-shirts. I think that's all they cared about."

Brodie tossed a mesh bag filled with black-and-white soccer balls toward the cabin door. "I figured as much." He looked at Haley. "Speaking of excited, Eli got pretty excited when he saw you here. The guys from his cabin should be getting off the bus next. They were gathering their gear from the back. I'm sure he'll make a beeline over here to find out how Buddy is doing. He hasn't stopped talking about that puppy. I'm hoping you're here with good news?"

Haley lifted the backpack. "I'm actually here to return this. But I wanted to give him an update on Buddy, too."

"So, how is he?" Brodie asked, climbing the porch steps to stand next to his wife. He wrapped an arm around her and she smiled up at him.

Haley swallowed. They reminded her of her parents back when things were still good, and of the kind of relationship she'd always thought she'd have.

"Buddy?" Savvy asked him. "I didn't realize we knew his name. Was he wearing a collar?"

"No," Haley said, "but apparently Gavin named him when they found him."

"Did he, now?" Savvy asked with a grin.

"From what he told me earlier, it wasn't intentional," Brodie said with a chuckle. "But, anyway, how's he doing?"

"He's doing…" Haley paused. She didn't want to say something that wasn't true, and the little dog was a far cry from being out of the woods. "He's doing okay."

Brodie's mouth slid down and he gave her a single nod. "Well, we'll just have to pray for him to be doing better than okay soon," he said as Haley saw Eli hop off the bus, with Gavin right behind him. They wore bright blue T-shirts that matched those of the other boys currently climbing out of the bus.

Eli said something to Gavin and then took off running toward Haley. She smiled at the boy but kept an eye on the big man also making his way toward Brodie and Savvy's front porch.

In addition to the bright blue T-shirt, Gavin Thomason wore well-worn jeans and tennis shoes. Nothing overly fancy, for sure, and similar to what Brodie and the other cabin counselors wore. But on Gavin, with the T-shirt accenting the firm, broad planes of his chest and shoulders, coupled with the jeans outlining lean hips and long legs, he looked more like a walking advertisement for an outdoor apparel store.

She caught herself staring, which really couldn't be prevented. He was just so easy on the eyes. But she glanced away in time to see that Savvy hadn't missed her reaction. One corner of her mouth had curved upward and Haley did her best to act like she hadn't noticed.

"Miss Haley! Did you bring Buddy? Is he better already?" Eli's feet slid to a stop near the bottom of the porch steps, where he dropped his jacket, mittens and bright yellow shin guards that matched his soccer cleats. "Did you? Is he here?"

She was grateful the sweet boy interrupted the uncomfortable moment and, hearing the hope in his tone, almost hated showing him the backpack. "Buddy is still at my office so I can take care of him, but I did bring you this." She held up the bag. "I thought you could use it for school tomorrow."

His expression fell in one big swoop. "Oh. Okay."

Gavin neared the porch, his jaw set firm and those intense blue eyes focusing on the little boy, barely acknowledging Haley or the other adults. "Eli, we talked about how it would take some time for Buddy to get better, right?"

"Yes, sir," Eli said solemnly, climbing the steps toward Haley. "Thank you for bringing my backpack."

"You're welcome." She couldn't stand the sadness in his face, or his tone, so she added, "And I look forward to you coming tomorrow afternoon to visit Buddy. I know he'll be happy to see you."

As she'd hoped, his mouth eased into a slight smile, full cheeks lifting with the action. "I will be happy to see him, too." Then his eyebrows inched up and he asked, "Hey, can you take him something for me, Miss Haley?"

"Take Buddy something?" She saw Brodie and Gavin exchange a look. "Um, sure. I'd be happy to. What do you have for him?"

Eli unzipped the backpack and rummaged through binders and papers until he found what he was looking for. A small library book. "I get to check out two books, 'cause I'm in the second grade. I can keep one for me to read, and you can take this one to read to him, if he wants to hear a story before he goes to bed."

Haley squatted to be eye to eye with the little boy. "Eli, that's so sweet. But I don't want to mess up your library book."

"You'll be careful." He put the book in her hand.

She glanced up to catch Savvy holding a hand to her chest. "You're right… I will be careful. And I'll read it to him tonight, when I go back to check on him."

"You promise?"

No way could she let him down. "I promise."

"It's a chapter book. You might not be able to read it all to him tonight, but you can do your best."

Haley was instantly reminded of her words to Gavin earlier, that she would do her best to heal the puppy. She glanced up to see his stern expression and assumed he recalled the same statement. "Yes, I will."

"I'll show you my favorite part." He opened the book.

That's when she noticed his hands, not moving as easily as she'd have expected for a boy his age. Then she saw the wrinkled skin across the top. When he turned the pages, she also noticed the fingers that weren't quite complete, the skin and bone melded together to join digits that should have been separate.

Her breath caught in her throat and she looked up to see Gavin, those blue eyes staring directly at her, telling her without words that she should maintain her composure…for Eli's sake.

Eli, swiftly moving through the pages despite his gnarled hands, smiled broadly when he got to the one he wanted. "This part. It's about when the boy finds his dog, like when I found Buddy."

Haley didn't know how much more her heart could take. She forced a smile. "I'll be sure to read that part to him."

Eli handed over the book, wrapped both arms around her and gave her a hug. "Thank you, Miss Haley. I'll see you tomorrow."

She inhaled the outdoorsy scent of a boy who'd been running on the soccer field, a combination of a little sweat, a lot of dirt and an abundance of…adorable. She squeezed a hug in return. "I can't wait to see you again, Eli."

And she meant every word.

"Okay, then—" Gavin ran a palm across the top of Eli's head "—you should go get your shower and get ready for bed now."

"You'll come read some more to us before we go to bed, Mr. Gavin?"

"I always do." Gavin reached out and ruffled Eli's hair as he walked away. The boy grinned back at the man who undeniably held a special spot in his world.

Regardless of his gruffness, he had such a soft spot for that child.

"I should start getting the guys moving toward bed," he said, nodding his goodbye and then turning to follow Eli toward the cabin.

But Haley couldn't end her day without knowing what happened to that poor child. "Wait!"

Gavin didn't need this, not today. But he'd seen the moment Haley Calhoun had noticed Eli's hands and he'd prayed she wouldn't want to discuss it.

But his heart had told him that she would.

Why hadn't she asked Savvy or Brodie? And why hadn't he made it to his cabin before she'd called out to stop his retreat from the attractive—and unnerving— woman?

Bracing himself as her footsteps approached, he stopped and turned to face her. "Yes?"

She glanced behind her toward Brodie and Savvy, now standing in front of their cabin speaking to several of the teen boys. "Can we talk in private for a moment?"

*No.* That was what he wanted to say. Not only because there weren't a whole lot of private places to talk at Willow's Haven—it was always saturated with kids and counselors, one of the things Gavin liked about working there—but also because he didn't want to be anywhere private with Haley Calhoun.

Or any other woman, for that matter.

However, he also didn't want to explain that, nor did he want to appear rude, when she was clearly concerned for Eli.

"We can sit at the fire pit for a moment," he conceded. "But I'll need to get my cabin ready for bed soon." Without waiting for a response, he started toward the circle of wooden benches and stumps surrounding the devotion area. She walked in silence beside him, but in spite of the lack of communication, he could sense the tension, the undeniable anxiety in the way she moved, and he dreaded the upcoming conversation. Eli had hit his own heart hard, and it'd be difficult explaining the boy's past without enlightening her to his own.

But he also knew she wouldn't leave without knowing. That was the way women were. They cared too much. Needed to know too much. Pulled at a man's heartstrings…too much.

Instead of taking a seat on one of the benches, which might have caused her to sit beside him, he selected one of the larger stumps. He watched as she took a bench nearby, sitting slowly and then rubbing her hands down the sides of her jeans.

Gavin waited for her to say something. But she merely sat there, looking nervous and like…she might cry.

*No, God. I can't handle this today and You know it. Help me out here, Lord. Let her say whatever she needs to say, learn whatever she needs to learn…and let me be.*

He cleared his throat. "What did you need, Dr. Calhoun?" The abrupt tone returned, but he couldn't help it. Maybe that would cause this conversation to end quickly.

She shivered, even though there wasn't any sign of a chill in the air. "What…happened to Eli?" Her hands flattened over her knees, fingers tightening as though visibly steadying herself for his answer.

Gavin thought of the boy, so loving and trusting, regardless of every letdown in his past. He'd known what she would ask, but that didn't make telling her any easier. He inhaled, let it out.

"He was at home with his parents, a little over a year ago, and they were all sleeping when their house caught fire." His mind painted a picture of Eli amid those burning flames.

One of her hands moved to her throat and the other to her stomach. "They—didn't make it out? His parents didn't make it?"

He shook his head. "Neighbors called 9-1-1. The firemen were able to get to Eli, but the house started caving in and they couldn't get to his parents." He ran a hand across his mouth, hating the truth of Eli's past. "From what we know, he somehow got free of his rescuers and ran back to the house, trying to get inside and save them."

"That's what happened to his hands?" Her voice was thick and raspy, filled with the same emotion Gavin experienced every time he thought about what Eli had been through at merely six years old. "He burned his hands trying to save his parents?"

He nodded, cleared his throat again and stood. "Eli needs that puppy to be okay. He *can't* lose someone else he was trying to save."

Gavin turned away before he saw her response. He hadn't wanted to hear the soft sob that tore from her throat. But he did. She was hurting for Eli and he under-

stood why. However, it wasn't his place to comfort Haley
Calhoun. Or any other female.

He couldn't go there.

Not today.

Not ever.

## Chapter Four

"We'd like you to head up the Adopt-an-Animal program, Gavin." Brodie glanced up from the sheet of notes he held in front of his breakfast plate. "It makes sense, with you already establishing a rapport with Dr. Calhoun."

Gavin had thought this morning's staff planning breakfast would be like any other: going over the week's activities, conveying issues concerning the children in their care and discussing current projects at Willow's Haven.

Which, of course, was what Brodie was doing now. Gavin simply hadn't realized *he* was on today's agenda.

He swallowed the bite of scrambled eggs that had tasted good a moment ago but now moved past his throat in a thick lump.

"I don't know that I've established a good rapport, necessarily." He didn't want to let Brodie and Savvy down if they'd selected him to run the program, but there had to be some other program he could run instead.

Unfortunately he couldn't think of a decent alternative to recommend.

Brodie grabbed a corner of toast and pointed it toward Gavin. "Now that you have those daily visits with Eli lined up, to take care of the puppy and all, we thought you might as well go ahead and meet with Dr. Calhoun about the program. Be her key point of contact for the activities and keep us aware of what she has planned for us at Willow's Haven, as well as at the Cutter farm."

"She'd mentioned the kids going to the Cutter Ranch to hike and spend time with the horses there as part of the program," Savvy added, "in addition to her bringing animals here for the children, and we think that's a great idea."

Obviously they'd put a lot of thought into this and Gavin should be happy to lead one of the programs. As a matter of fact, at last week's staff breakfast meeting, he'd asked for more responsibility at the children's home.

Now he was getting it.

But that meant spending additional time with Haley Calhoun.

"Sounds like a good idea to me," Mark mumbled beside him. His grin said he didn't mind Gavin's discomfort with the notion.

Gavin leaned toward his fellow counselor. "Did you tell them they should put me in charge of this?"

Mark popped a couple of red grapes into his mouth, smiling as he chewed. "Not me—" he held up his hands, palms forward "—but it does seem like a good idea, given your good rapport with the pretty vet and all."

"I don't have a good—"

"Gavin? Can you do this for us?" Brodie said from the other end of the dining table, Savvy smiling reassuringly beside her husband.

As reluctant as he was to team up with Haley, Gavin couldn't deny that he wanted to do whatever he could to help them succeed in their goals for the kids.

"I can," he said at last.

"Great." Brodie popped the rest of the toast in his mouth, chewed and swallowed. "We talked to Haley about it this morning, and we'd like you to go meet with her. She said she would be available most of the day."

Not what Gavin wanted to hear, but since he had to see her later anyway… "I can speak with her when I take Eli to visit Buddy."

"She wanted to spend a bit more time with you than that, I think," Savvy said. "She mentioned y'all deciding which animals to bring, setting up the groups of kids, scheduling dates for traveling to the Cutter Ranch and so on. We were hoping you could meet during the day, while the kids are at school, so y'all could have more time to iron out all the details."

More time with Haley Calhoun? Again, not what he wanted.

"I can call her. We can discuss it over the phone, I'm sure," he offered. When he watched Brodie and Savvy exchange a disappointed look at his suggestion, he added, "Or I could ride over there after we get done with this meeting."

Gavin knew that would be better, instead of him trying to cover the program information over the phone, but he wasn't all that keen on more one-on-one time with Haley. Their brief interaction at the fire pit last night had left him more uncomfortable than he cared to admit. In fact, he'd awakened this morning thinking he should have turned around when he'd heard her crying.

But he'd walked away.

"That'd be great," Brodie said, moving on to the next topic of discussion.

Haley gently pinched the skin behind Buddy's neck between her thumb and forefinger and frowned as the tiny tuft stayed tented before gradually returning into place. She'd started him on a slow IV for fluid replacement therapy last night and had hoped for a better response by this morning.

"Come on, little guy." She tenderly stroked the brittle fur on his back. "Eli needs you to be okay."

Buddy squinted one eye to look at her, then closed it, as if he didn't have the energy to respond. He hadn't minded the IV, hadn't squirmed when she'd checked his vitals, hadn't done much of anything this morning.

Which didn't do a thing to alleviate Haley's concerns.

She'd even called Doc Sheridan to get his advice on how to handle the tiny puppy, and he'd concluded that she was doing everything he would've done. Which also didn't sit well. She would have loved to have heard of something she'd forgotten, some minor detail that would cause Buddy to take a turn for the better, preferably before Eli came to visit.

She updated his chart, then glanced at the library book Eli had given her yesterday afternoon. As promised, she'd read the story to Buddy last night. Even though it was a "chapter book," she'd finished the entire thing, not because she'd thought Buddy wanted to hear it, but because it made her feel good to know she was doing something Eli wanted.

Roscoe barked from the next room, which set off a string of happy yelps and barks from Honey and Sugar in the adjoining kennels. She'd placed Buddy away from the others to keep him in the quietest spot possible, but now she opened the door so the boarded animals could see they weren't alone. As she suspected, the barking settled down to happy yips.

A bell dinged as the front door opened.

"Dr. Calhoun? It's Gavin Thomason. Are you here? I need to speak to you." The tone was stiff and sharp, as though he couldn't wait to get the conversation over with…or as though hoping she wasn't around.

"Bad news for him," she said to Buddy. "I'm here." She rubbed a finger beneath his chin then closed the gate to the kennel. "What could have gone so badly in his past to make him such a bear?"

She walked to the lobby and found the brooding grizzly looking as appealing as yesterday in a bright blue pullover, jeans and hiking boots. And while she'd thought she may have imagined how muscular he'd seemed before, now she easily verified she hadn't missed the mark.

He was as fit as she'd thought.

And as handsome.

And as dark and broody.

Savvy had said he'd been through a lot in his past. Even though Haley had no idea what, she'd give him the benefit of the doubt and attempt to be cordial. She managed a smile. "Hello, Mr. Thomason. I was just checking on Buddy in the back."

His brow furrowed. "Is he not doing well?"

And there was the doubt in her abilities once more.

Haley swallowed past the urge to snarl. "He's a little better than yesterday. Still not great, but he's only getting started absorbing liquids."

He took a deep breath and let it out. "Okay, good."

Haley waited a beat and, feeling awkward at the tension caused by his mere presence, asked, "Was there something else you needed?"

"Brodie and Savvy wanted me to meet with you about the new program."

"Oh, right. She told me you would be my contact for Willow's Haven. I'd hoped we could get everything organized today and start the program this week."

His eyes widened slightly, brow furrowed again. "Right. Well, anyway, I made a list of kids in each cabin and divided them into groups that should be manageable when you bring the animals to the home and when they travel to the Cutter farm." He pulled several folded pieces of paper from his back pocket.

A loud meow echoed down the hallway and she turned toward the sound. "Oh, that's my phone."

"Your phone?"

"I have animal ringtones. It probably isn't important, but you never know. Do you mind if I take the call?"

Both eyebrows lifted, blue eyes studying her as though she was the most bizarre female on the planet simply because she had animal ringtones. But he nodded. "Go ahead."

She held up a finger. "I'll be right back." She darted toward Doc Sheridan's old office, where she kept her personal belongings, the meowing growing louder with every ring.

Most of her clients dialed the landline unless they had an emergency after hours, so she assumed this was probably either her mother checking in or her grandfather just wanting to chat. If so, she'd let them know she had someone in the office and that she'd call them back.

But when she looked at the Caller ID on the display, she saw Landon Cutter's name.

"Hey, Landon, Roscoe will be ready to pick up any-time you like," she said upon answering.

"Haley, it's Georgiana. Landon dialed your number and then handed me the phone while he's with Brownie in the barn. I'm sorry to bother you but…we're…having a difficult time."

Georgiana was Landon's wife. Though she was quite capable of doing pretty much anything, she was blind, which explained his dialing the number and handing her the phone.

"What's going on with Brownie?" Abi's favorite horse was due to foal in two weeks.

Georgiana's voice quivered as she spoke. "She's drop-ping her foal now, Haley. It's too early, so Landon's wor-ried. I am, too. Thankfully, Abi is at school, so she doesn't know what's happening. Can you get here? Soon?"

A swift kick of adrenaline swept through Haley's veins while she pivoted and grabbed the emergency farm call bag. "I'm on my way."

"Do you think the foal will be okay this time, Haley? I mean, it coming this early—that isn't good, is it?"

"Mares can successfully foal outside of the typical gestation range," Haley said, reciting what she knew to be true even if not always likely. She'd been with Doc Sheridan last year when Brownie had lost her first foal, and she'd seen Abi's tears.

As well as Landon's and Georgiana's.

She sure didn't want to experience them going through that again.

Georgiana sniffed through the line. "Okay, then, maybe everything will be okay. I'll start praying."

The urge to say she'd pray, as well, pushed at Haley's lips, but she swallowed past it. "I'll be there soon."

Bag in hand, she started for the door…and nearly

ran smack-dab into the intimidating male currently claiming dominion in her lobby.

Gavin hadn't meant to eavesdrop, but the vet's voice had echoed down the hall. It appeared there was a problem with someone's pet.

He hoped the animal was okay, but he also didn't mind that the problem might cause them to postpone this meeting. Maybe the next time he came to meet with the doctor, her assistant would be around and he wouldn't find himself alone—again—with Haley Calhoun.

She reentered the lobby wide-eyed and looking frazzled, a large black satchel draped over one shoulder. At some point during her phone call, her ponytail had started falling, leaving her hair semicontained, blond wisps tumbling past her delicate cheekbones. "Oh!" she gasped, as though she'd forgotten leaving him here while she'd chased after a meowing cell phone.

"Everything okay?" He suspected that whatever had her darting out would most definitely keep him from having to meet with her today.

Worked for Gavin.

"Oh, yes—" She shook her head. "No. No, everything isn't okay, or it might not be. I need to go." She started toward the door then paused to face him. "But I don't want to wait any longer to get the program started at Willow's Haven. Come with me. We can talk on the way."

"Come—with you?" He'd only met the lady yesterday, had been forced to work with her today, and now... she wanted him to head to who-knew-where with her.

"Yes, please." She didn't wait for his answer, just opened the door for him to exit.

He followed her outside.

She slammed the door behind them and continued toward her truck, leaving a distinctive scent of apples and cinnamon in her wake.

Gavin remained rock solid on the front porch as she hurried to her pickup. Casting a glance over her shoulder, she crossed the front of the truck then swished her hair from her face with her fingertips. "Never mind. I have to go. We can meet tomorrow," she called across the windshield. Then she opened the driver's-side door and started climbing in.

Without taking the time to second-guess his actions, Gavin sprinted toward the passenger's side of the truck and got in. "So, where are we going?"

She grabbed the keys from the cup holder, fumbling with them before dropping them near his feet on the passenger floorboard.

They reached down at the same time, feminine hands with long fingers connecting with his forearm instead of the keys, already captured between his thumb and forefinger. He glanced at her, found her way too close for comfort, and caught another tantalizing whiff of apples and cinnamon.

"Sorry," she said, near enough that he felt her breath against his lips.

He moved the keys to her hand and released his hold on the key ring, waiting for her to move away. "No problem."

Ignoring the odd interaction, she straightened in her seat and pushed the key into the ignition. "We're going to the Cutter farm."

He'd heard a lot about the place but hadn't been there. "Where we'll be taking the kids to hike and to ride horses?"

"Yes." The engine whirred to life. "And where one of those horses lost her very first colt last year and is now dropping her foal too early. We're going to try and make sure it's okay."

Gavin's mind reeled, the awkward feeling of being close enough to kiss Haley Calhoun swiftly replaced by an even more unpleasant scenario. "Dropping her foal," he said, pretty sure that meant…

"Having her baby."

His stomach pitched as he honed in on the key word in her proclamation.

"*We're* going to make sure the baby is okay?"

The truck lurched as she stomped on the gas. "I meant *I'm* going to make sure. I'm just used to having someone with me. Last year, I rode with Doc Sheridan when Brownie dropped her foal. This year, you're going with me."

"The difference being you are a vet and I'm not," he pointed out, grabbing the door handle as she accelerated.

She glanced his way as the truck jerked onto the main road and Gavin saw the slight hint of a smile curl the corners of those pink-glossed lips. "Don't worry. I don't expect you to help deliver the foal. I just asked you to come along because I don't want to wait any longer to start the program for Eli and the other kids at Willow's Haven, and we can discuss it on the way to the farm."

"Where you're planning to deliver a horse."

"Well, Brownie has already gotten started with the delivery. I'm going because she's early and Landon and Georgiana obviously think something isn't right."

Gavin examined her hands flexing against the steering wheel. Was *that* why she looked so jittery? Because she was afraid something wasn't right? Surely, assist-

ing an animal giving birth fell into her job description. But she didn't act as though this was anything usual.

Gavin thought he knew why. "You said she lost her baby last year?"

The smile evaporated as quickly as it came. "Yeah, and that would've been her first. Landon and Georgiana's eleven-year-old daughter, Abi, was devastated. I don't want her—or her parents—to go through that again. And I sure don't want to lose this baby my first week as Claremont's only vet."

"How early is the baby?" He worked to put the pieces into place, preferably before they arrived at the farm, which should happen soon at this speed.

She blew out a breath, sending more blond wisps tumbling against her face. He tried to ignore the way it made him notice her jawline and slender neck.

"Two weeks." She pressed harder on the gas.

Gavin wondered how two weeks early affected a horse giving birth, but from the way Haley continued to sling him sideways on every curve and the manner in which she chewed nervously on her bottom lip…it wasn't good.

Memories of his own mad dash toward an impending birth slammed him with as much force as Haley's frantic driving.

But were much more painful.

Selah's tears slipping down her cheeks as he'd driven madly to get her to the hospital.

*Everything will be okay*, she'd said. *Lots of babies come early and are just fine.* He could almost see her sucking in a deep breath as a massive contraction hit and then squinting through the pain. *Right?*

Gavin closed his eyes, fought the pull of his tears, itching for release, and swallowed past the urge to

vomit, the torment of that day wreaking havoc not only
on his body but on his soul.

Because he suddenly remembered how very much
he'd despised God at that moment.

"I hate to think how this will hit Abi if I can't save
that baby," Haley said.

Gavin recalled the doctors working to keep his wife
alive. And then their son. He'd distinctly heard a young
nurse's voice, her panic barely controlled as she yelled,
"We're losing her!"

Gavin had been there, listening. Praying. He'd always planned to be in the delivery room, to see his baby
born and then…everything went wrong.

Instead of accompanying her into the delivery room
the way they'd planned, a flurry of doctors and nurses
filled the area, arms pushing him toward the hall, telling him he would have to wait outside.

The door closing.

Gavin still listening. And praying.

Then, when the doctor confirmed that Selah was
gone…

Screaming.

At God.

"I just don't know what Abi will do if this baby dies,
too," Haley continued.

It'd taken him a long time to determine that God
hadn't been the enemy that day and that He had never
left Gavin. In fact, He had seen Gavin through the dark
time that followed and helped him to find his way to
Willow's Haven. And now, when a little girl could lose
a baby that *she* very much wanted, Gavin knew Who
to turn to. "I'll pray."

Haley shot him a quick glance, eyebrows dipping.
Then she inhaled, exhaled and said resignedly, "Thanks."

By the time Gavin silently said, "Amen," they were turning onto a dirt road beneath a wooden sign with Cutter Ranch and Fish Camp etched in its center. She slowed the truck to navigate the bumpy road, but her breathing increased to the point that he thought she might hyperventilate.

"Gavin?" she asked as they passed colorful cabins beside a lake that he assumed formed the Fish Camp portion of the farm.

He noticed she no longer looked at him but kept her vision straight ahead as she spoke. "Yeah?"

"I totally forgot to have you read over your lists of Willow's Haven kids to me while we were driving."

"With the way you were driving, I'm not sure I'd have been able to read them anyway," he said, attempting to lighten the tension within the truck. He was certain she had no idea how much this trip, this situation, affected him, too, and he sure didn't plan to tell her. "We can go over the lists later."

Her mouth lifted in a smile and she glanced at him, green eyes sparkling. "Yeah, I guess you're right."

The truck jutted to the left when she hit a rock, and she turned her attention to the large red barn centering two log cabins in front of them.

The smile disintegrated. "Gavin?"

"Yeah?"

"Did you? Pray?" Her mouth wobbled after the last word.

"I did."

She nodded, as though she'd expected nothing less. "Thank you. I…think I might need it."

He opened his mouth, almost told her that everything was going to be okay, but then remembered those very words coming from so many people while he'd awaited news of Selah and their baby.

None of them had been true.

So he prayed again, that everything *would* be okay, and that they were about to experience something wonderful… rather than something horrific.

If anyone knew a birth could go either way, it was Gavin.

## Chapter Five

Haley's palms clenched the steering wheel, her heart beating so fiercely she could feel her pulse in her ears. Her every fear of failing as a vet pierced her spirit with a vengeance. What if this baby *didn't* make it?

She saw Georgiana, elbows braced on jeans-clad knees, hands tunneling through her long, auburn hair as she sat on an old wooden bench at this end of the barn. Haley parked her pickup next to Landon's and gathered her courage. "I can do this." She hardly noticed she'd made the statement aloud until Gavin answered.

"Yes, you can. It's what you were trained to do, isn't it?" His jaw tensed as he peered toward the barn, as if he knew all the potential scenarios—potential problems—she could encounter. "They're counting on you to do your job."

She took a deep breath, turned off the ignition and grabbed her bag. "Right." Then she climbed out and headed toward the barn without waiting for him to exit. She had no idea how involved he'd want to be in this house call, and she probably shouldn't have suggested he ride along, but she'd been so eager to discuss the program.

And then so absorbed in the task at hand that they hadn't even mentioned it.

Even so, she heard his truck door shut behind her as she hurried toward Georgiana. She wondered if he'd end up having to witness her falling apart if this didn't go well. She should have suggested he follow her in his vehicle.

She reached the barn and all worries about Gavin Thomason were forgotten. Scents of the barn, fresh hay, sweet feed and horses, filled the air.

But something else filled the air, as well, and Haley recognized it instantly…

Fear.

Had they already lost the foal?

Georgiana stood, her face tense and eyes red-rimmed. "Haley?"

"Yes, it's me, and Gavin Thomason from Willow's Haven," she answered quickly. "How's Brownie?"

Georgiana tilted her head at the opposite side of the barn. "Landon is in the birthing stall with her. He just yelled that it's getting near the twenty-minute mark and that the foal needs to be repositioned. Something's not right. I think he was going to try to do it himself if you didn't get here in time. I'm—so glad you're here."

"Okay." Haley did her best to keep her voice calm and assured. She turned to Gavin. "You stay here with Georgiana, and I'll call for you if I need you."

His face lost a little of its color, but he moved toward Georgiana. "Okay."

Haley hurried to the birthing stall. *I can do this, I can do this*, she silently repeated. Taking one last glance at Gavin, now seated beside Georgiana on the bench, she added, *I'm…really glad he came.*

She wasn't sure whether she felt that way because

she didn't want to be there alone or because she knew he'd prayed for the outcome when she simply couldn't talk that way to God anymore. In any case, she truly was glad that Gavin Thomason was there.

And she hoped when she saw him again, she'd be sharing news of a precious new foal.

Gavin watched her disappear into the largest stall at the opposite end of the barn. He heard Landon speaking rapidly, bringing her up to speed on what had happened since Georgiana had called the clinic.

His mind flashed to the rapid voices of the doctors and nurses trying to save his wife and child.

Then he heard Haley, her tone calm and comforting as she apparently took over with whatever they were doing in the stall. She sounded confident, capable... ready.

Gavin said another prayer.

A loud snort, followed by a miserable moan from the troubled horse, suddenly took precedence over all other sounds.

"You're...Haley's friend?" Georgiana asked.

Gavin knew she talked to keep her mind off the spine-chilling sounds at the other end of the barn. Since talking might also enable him to stop replaying the most tormenting moments of his life, he concentrated on engaging in conversation instead of listening to Brownie's excruciating groans.

"I actually just met Dr. Calhoun yesterday," he said, then added, "and you and I have met before, at church." It was true that he didn't have a great memory for people's names, as he'd showed yesterday with Aaliyah, but he did recall meeting the blind woman and her husband.

A bellowing groan echoed through the barn and

Georgiana winced before answering, "Right. I remember Savvy introducing you a few weeks back. You're the new counselor." She said the words, but her attention was obviously still on Brownie.

"Yes, I am."

A lengthy, agonizing, rumbling snort, combined with Haley's brisk instructions and Landon's responses, filled the barn. It was useless to try to talk about anything else, so he said the first thing that came to mind.

"Everything will be okay."

His throat clenched as soon as the words were out.

He'd *promised* himself he'd never repeat that phrase, because he knew firsthand it might not be true. And he suddenly realized that, when all those people had told him the same thing two years ago...that may have been all they could think to say.

Gavin instantly regretted the animosity he'd felt toward those people. They'd undoubtedly hoped that everything *would* be okay with his wife and baby.

But nothing had ever been "okay" again.

He rubbed his hand down his face, grateful Georgiana couldn't see his anguish.

"I'm praying you're right," she said. "Because last year, when she lost her colt, we were heartbroken. And Abi has been so hopeful for this baby. She prays for it every morning and every night." Georgiana's head fell back to rest against the barn wall, her top teeth grazing her lower lip as she shook her head. "I hate this feeling I have, that..."

Gavin waited a beat, heard another spine-chilling moan from the other end of the barn, then asked, "That... what?"

"That it'd be better if Doc Sheridan were here. I mean, we like Haley—Dr. Calhoun—and we trust her and all, but Doc Sheridan has *always* been our vet, and she's much younger. I don't know how she is in an emergency on her own. And this baby is so important to Abi…"

Gavin had told her the truth; he'd met Haley only yesterday. However, in that brief time, he'd seen how much she cared about Eli and that pitiful puppy and witnessed her reaction to seeing Eli's injury.

Moreover, he'd observed firsthand how desperately she wanted to save this baby in her frantic drive over and in the way she resolved herself to do her job when they'd arrived at the barn.

"She may be younger, but she cares about her patients and she's been in practice with Doc Sheridan. She's taking the best possible care of Brownie and that baby. I'm sure of it."

"I know you're right," Georgiana whispered. "It's just so hard to keep my faith when last year everything ended so suddenly. That baby didn't make it a day."

Gavin's own baby hadn't made it a day, either. He swallowed past that bitter pill. "I've been praying."

"Thank you," she said. "I have, too."

A movement at the back of the barn caught Gavin's attention and he looked up to see Landon, smiling, stepping from the stall. He turned toward a large barrel trash can and removed arm-length gloves. Haley, however, already stood halfway between the rear of the barn and the front, not too far from where he and Georgiana sat. She dropped a ball of plastic that Gavin presumed to be her own gloves in another barrel, then moved to a large mud sink to wash her hands.

"Georgiana," Landon said, squeezing Haley's shoulder as he passed her on his walk toward his wife.

"Landon? What is it? What happened?" She stood

from the bench while her husband moved closer and wrapped his arms around her.

"Everything is okay," he said softly. "Little filly was a bit stubborn, but thanks to Dr. Calhoun, she's doing just fine."

"A filly." Georgiana sucked in a breath and rubbed her face against his chest before releasing a fresh batch of tears. "Abi—is going to be so happy." She sniffed, brushed her fingers across her cheeks. "And, Haley, thank you. I was so worried, but I'm so very grateful."

Haley smiled at Georgiana as she moved closer, but her eyes were locked with Gavin's. "I'm just doing what I was trained for, but this is one of the best parts of being a vet, helping a life begin."

"Come on, sweetheart," Landon said, leading Georgiana toward the birthing stall. "I'll take you back there. Brownie is standing, and the baby will be soon. I can give you a play-by-play as it happens."

"That'd be wonderful." She leaned against him as they walked toward the rear of the barn.

"You're sticking around a little while, right, Doc Calhoun?" Landon asked. "Just to make sure everything's fine?"

"Of course," she answered. "I'll give you two a little time with them, and then I'll be right there. Just yell if you need me sooner."

"You got it."

Gavin watched her, more of her hair escaping the ponytail and framing her face, her green eyes electric with excitement. And her smile didn't quit.

He'd thought she was stunning before, but right now she was breathtaking.

"Hey," she said as she drew closer, "I want to thank you for that."

"Thank me? For what?"

"I heard what you said to Georgiana when she was doubting my abilities." She lifted a shoulder. "I can't say that I blame her. Between you and me, that was the first horse birth I've handled on my own."

"I just told her what I believed to be true."

"Yesterday, with Buddy, you sounded a lot like her," she pointed out. "What changed?"

He hadn't even thought of that, but she was right. "I got to see the good doctor in action. I saw how determined you were to take care of that baby."

"Well, it meant a lot to me."

"So Brownie and the filly…" he said gruffly "…they're both okay?"

"Better than okay. And that little filly is absolutely beautiful, already holding her head up and sniffing her mom. She should stand and then hopefully nurse soon. That's what her last baby wouldn't do, no matter how hard we tried to help. But this baby… She was a little stubborn, needed some assistance, but then everything went so amazingly well. It was—" her eyes blinked rapidly "—unbelievable."

He could hear Georgiana's exclamations of awe and wonder from the other end of the barn. "So you'll go check on the baby again before we go?"

She nodded. "I will. I'd like to wait until we see that she'll nurse before we head out. Is that okay with you? Do you have time to stay?"

He nodded. "I'm good until the kids get back from school."

"Great. Well, we shouldn't be here too much longer, then we can hopefully discuss the program and schedule our first outings with the animals."

"Sounds good," he said. Thinking about the new

baby at the back of the barn, he asked, "Do you think they'd mind if I joined you, when you check on her?"

"I'm sure they wouldn't mind at all."

As if on cue, Landon leaned out of the stall. "Y'all want to come see them? The baby's standing."

Haley's smile crept into her cheeks. "Awesome. Yes, we do," she said.

To Gavin's surprise, she took his hand, the warmth of her delicate palm pressing against his and reminding him…of every shattered dream. "Come on," she said softly, "you've got to see this beautiful baby."

Her words sliced at his heart, but Gavin walked alongside her and couldn't push away the memory of the first time he'd seen his beautiful baby boy. A headful of dark hair. Tiny little face. Fists balled as he fought for life.

"She's got the most incredible blaze markings," Haley said, explaining, "a wide white stripe down the middle of her face."

Gavin forced his thoughts from the baby of the past to the one of the present. He admired the pride Haley had in the foal she'd helped bring into the world. As they rounded the corner that put them at the gated opening to the birthing stall, he saw why.

Landon and Georgiana stood off to one side so that Haley and Gavin got a front-row seat to the action: the filly taking her first steps.

Like Haley had mentioned, she had a wide white stripe down her face. The remainder of her body was the same deep chestnut as her mother, except for her mane, which was the same stark white as the blaze down her face.

"Wow," Gavin whispered as long, spindly legs bowed

a little while the newborn attempted to figure out what to do with them.

Protectively circling her baby, Brownie gave a soft, low whinny that Gavin hadn't heard before.

"That's her maternal nicker." Haley's eyes misted as she watched the motherly gesture. "It's her way of telling the baby to move closer."

And the filly certainly seemed to understand, shakily moving those long limbs to get nearer to her mother. She fell, the soft hay swooshing with her defeat, but Brownie dipped her head low and nudged the babe while continuing to make the sound that told the filly to get close.

Gavin held his breath as the baby tried, only to fall again. He wanted to intervene, and he could tell every other adult in the stall did, too, but they all knew to simply watch and wait.

With another coaxing from her mother, the filly gave a valiant effort and, though her legs looked as though they would buckle, she put one hoof in front of the other and found her way to her mother's milk.

"She's found her," Landon whispered to Georgiana.

"Is she nursing?" Georgiana returned.

The nearly inaudible sucking sounds gave her the answer she wanted. The baby had found what she needed for survival. Her mother.

Gavin stood in amazement, releasing his heavy breath. "She's—going to be okay then?" he asked Haley.

She nodded. "I do believe she is."

Landon hugged Georgiana again and then crossed the stall to hug Haley, too. "Thank you, Doc Calhoun. You…can't know how much this means to us."

"It means as much to me," she answered.

Landon cupped a hand to Gavin's arm. "Glad you were here for this. Pretty incredible, huh?"

Gavin nodded, raw emotions hitting him full force. *This* was what he should've experience two years ago. Excitement. A stirring in his heart. In his soul. The incomparable awe of new life.

His jaw tensed, throat convulsed, eyes burned. If he stayed another minute, he'd lose it.

He turned and made his way to the truck.

## Chapter Six

Haley cast a concerned eye toward Gavin as they drove to the clinic. Not that he could see her. He was too focused on the papers in his hands…and avoiding eye contact with the woman driving the truck.

He hadn't mentioned what had happened when they'd seen the filly. Hadn't acknowledged the fact that he'd walked away midconversation, when they'd all been talking about their remarkable morning and how happy they were that the baby was okay.

In fact, he hadn't talked about anything except the new program.

Which was good, she supposed, because she wanted to finalize their plans and get the Adopt-an-Animal program started as soon as possible. But she also wanted to know the reason behind his odd behavior at the barn.

"My thoughts were that we could divide the kids up based on cabins. We have eight cabins with six children in each. When you bring animals to Willow's Haven, we can combine cabins, so that you'll have four groups of twelve."

"That sounds good. Can we start tomorrow?"

He didn't look away from the page. "The kids are

open tomorrow. No soccer practice or any other extracurricular activities. You're ready to bring the animals and get started?"

"Sure."

He made this seem like an interview rather than two people working together. After their conversation on the ride to the farm, and then the way he'd defended her abilities to Georgiana, she'd thought they'd finally turned a corner in their working relationship.

But then, after whatever had happened in the barn, he'd gone back to gruff and grumpy Gavin.

Which left Haley feeling more confused than ever.

"I'll let Brodie and Savvy know, so they can put it on tomorrow's schedule." He tapped his phone to send a text. "Would four thirty work? That should give the kids time to have their afternoon snack and at least get started on their homework before you get there."

"That's fine." Did he really think she wouldn't ask what had caused the sudden change in his demeanor?

He sent the text and pocketed his phone as they turned onto the road leading to the clinic. "Do you want to get in touch with Landon and Georgiana about scheduling some visits for the kids there, or would you like me to?" His tone was quick, clipped and precise, as though trying to get this over with and get away from her as soon as possible.

"I will ask if we can start those visits on the weekends. Maybe even this Saturday," she said. "I could've scheduled our first visit while we were there, but with all the excitement, I didn't think about it." She thought referencing the baby's birth would remind him of the wonderful morning they'd shared…until his abrupt exit.

"Okay." He folded the papers and pushed them into his jeans' pocket. "I think we've covered everything.

I'll head back when we get to the clinic. After Eli finishes his homework this afternoon, I'll bring him to see the puppy."

She'd pegged it right; he couldn't wait to leave.

In a moment they'd arrive at the clinic, she'd park, he'd get out…and she'd never learn what had gone wrong at the barn.

Huffing out a frustrated breath, she spotted one of the things she liked most about the lengthy driveway leading to the clinic. A small alcove canopied by mature oak trees. Often, when she took the boarded dogs on their nature walks, she would bring them here, sit at the pretty blue picnic table Doc Sheridan had left and think about life.

Today she saw the cozy haven as the perfect place to get some answers.

She pulled her truck into the recess, rolled down the windows and parked beneath the dappled blanket of red, gold and green leaves that hovered above the private space. Removing the key, she dropped it into the cup holder and shifted in the seat to face her passenger.

Turbulent blue eyes filled with confusion finally glanced her way. "Dr. Calhoun?" His tone, still gruff and clipped, only increased her determination.

"Haley," she corrected. "You should call me Haley. And we need to talk."

He turned to look ahead again, probably because he didn't want her to see his expression. Maybe he knew what she'd already determined—the man couldn't hide much in those telling eyes.

In the brief time she'd known him, she'd already recognized *doubt* when he'd first met her and didn't believe in her abilities, *compassion* when he was around Eli, *concern* when he thought something might be wrong with the baby, *excitement* when he learned the filly was okay and then *bewilderment* when she'd pulled into this alcove.

What she hadn't seen, however, were his eyes when he stormed out of that barn.

His back went rigid as he stared straight ahead. Even without him looking at her, she could still see his furrowed brow and clenched jaw. "*Haley*, we've covered everything we need to talk about today and I need to get back."

She knew better. He didn't *need* to get back; he needed to get away.

But she wasn't giving up that easily.

"Listen, if we're working on this program together, we'll be dealing with each other on a near-daily basis. I'll be honest—I wasn't thrilled about that after our first meeting, but then I could tell that you really cared about Eli and the other kids at Willow's Haven."

"I do," he said, using no more words than necessary.

She didn't stop. "Today, you were an entirely different person when we drove to the farm, like someone I'd actually like to have as a friend. But then you were downright rude and, for the life of me, I can't figure out why."

If possible, his jaw clenched tighter. Then he closed his eyes and leaned his head back against the seat.

Haley had no idea if he was praying…or counting to ten.

Either way, he'd ticked her off.

"Gavin, I'm *volunteering* my time for this program, and it's going to be a lot of time, from what I can tell. If I'm going to work with someone to pull this off, I'd much rather it be someone that is easy to get along with.

And who I don't have to walk on eggshells around because I have no idea what sets them off.

"Something bothered you at the barn. And whatever it was—whatever I did—can't be fixed if I don't know the problem."

He remained stone still. Eyes still closed. Jaw still clenched.

She took a deep breath…and counted to ten herself. "Maybe I should ask Brodie and Savvy if they can get someone else from Willow's Haven to work with me. If you don't want to…"

"No, I *want* to do this. And what happened at the barn had *nothing* to do with you," he growled, his tone filled with heated emotion.

How could she work with this bear of a man?

"I don't see how this can work." Surely there was another counselor who wouldn't be so difficult.

When he remained silent, she decided to put an end to what would surely be an uncomfortable alliance.

"For the past few years, all of my relationships with men haven't ended that well."

He remained silent but she noticed him flinch, as though bracing for an open-and-honest discussion. Maybe he wasn't used to that, but that was the only way Haley knew, so he might as well get ready.

"I know that's not the kind of relationship we'll have here—we're simply working together—but still… there's underlying tension between us that might negatively impact the program. Therefore, I think it might be better for everyone involved if my contact from Willow's Haven was one of the female counselors."

"I told you, what happened in the barn had nothing to do with you," he said, and she finally heard a hint of the compassion she'd witnessed from him last night when he'd told her Eli's story. "This was all about me. I was handling this morning okay, but then…I wasn't."

Haley was clueless. She had done her best to give him a way out of working with her and he wasn't taking it.

But at least he was starting to talk.

"What do you mean 'handling the morning okay'?"

Gavin had not planned to have this conversation today—or ever. Especially not with Haley Calhoun.

Or any other female.

But she'd misinterpreted his reaction to the new filly and, if he couldn't make her understand, she would ask for someone else to work with on the Adopt-an-Animal program. Even now, as she'd basically trapped him here in the truck for something akin to an interrogation, he knew she wanted only what was best for the kids. He'd seen firsthand what a caring person she was and he couldn't let her think *she'd* done anything wrong.

He turned to face her and found that she'd turned completely sideways, propped an elbow on the back of the seat and had her right knee resting on the middle bench. Nothing confrontational about her body language, but easily saying that she was willing to wait as long as it took for him to communicate.

No doubt about it, Haley Calhoun was different than anyone he'd met in a very long time. Most people avoided uncomfortable conversations. However this woman seemed to understand that getting to the truth often meant wading through rough, stormy waters.

He should know. Right now, he was drowning.

"Gavin?"

He cleared his throat. "A lot of things can go wrong when a baby is born."

"That's true. But the filly is fine. You saw that."

"And I was glad for it. But the whole thing… Being there and wondering if everything would be okay, and then the moment when I saw the baby standing by her mother, and seeing her mother taking care of her… It reminded me of the moments I never saw. Moments I never *will* see." The vision of the mare with her filly pierced his heart again. "And I had to leave."

Her lip slowly rolled in as she considered his words, eyes squinted in her confusion. Then her head shook slightly and she admitted, "I don't understand."

"Two years ago…" he started. "In fact, two years ago yesterday, my wife went into labor…ten weeks early."

"Your wife?"

He closed his eyes, remembered Selah's face, practically glowing when she'd told him she was pregnant. "Her name was Selah."

Haley's eyes softened, hand moving to her mouth as she realized what the past tense inferred. Gavin was used to the look. He'd received it often, especially when he'd still lived in Memphis around so many people who had known them as a couple.

"We knew something was wrong," he continued, "more than the baby coming early. Everything had been going well with the pregnancy, but then Selah had started hurting. Severe contractions that had her doubled over with pain. On the way to the hospital, she had the first seizure."

She whispered, "Eclampsia?"

He nodded. "Even when I knew something wasn't right, even when everything went completely opposite of how we'd planned, I thought she'd be okay." His chest constricted. "I prayed and prayed." He recalled his body collapsing, knees buckling and hitting the floor as he'd begged God not to take her. "But…she didn't make it."

Haley's head continued to shake, eyes watering. "I'm—so sorry." And then she zeroed in on the second excruciating part of that horrific day. "Gavin… what about the baby?"

He closed his eyes, vividly saw that doctor, blue scrubs and white surgical mask, walking purposefully toward him. "An hour later a doctor informed me that our baby was dying and that there was nothing they could do about it. It was the coldest, cruelest thing anyone has ever said to me. As if he didn't care that, when my wife and baby lost their lives…I also lost mine."

Her heart lurched painfully in her chest.

"They let me hold him. He was so very small, but his little fingers…moved to wrap around mine." His thumb inched across his first finger and he could almost see his son's fragile hand against his skin, could almost feel his feather-soft touch. "At that moment I thought maybe, somehow, he would pull through." He took a deep breath, let it out. "But then my son was gone."

Her tears spilled over. "I—I don't know what to say." She reached out to him, her hand touching his shoulder. "I'm so sorry. I was awful to you, and now I can see how the scare this morning, the rush to the farm and especially Brownie bonding with her baby, reminded you of everything you lost…" Her tears continued to fall. "Can you ever forgive me?"

Gavin had had many people express their sympathy, *say* they were sorry. But not a single one had actually pinpointed or observed why things that wouldn't bother someone else…speared his heart and soul.

Like the vision this morning in the barn.

"I forgive you."

One sharp bark was all the warning they had before an overly excited large dog bounded against the side of the truck, his head easily clearing the bottom of Haley's open window as he attempted to jump inside.

"Oh!" she yelled, turning toward the high-spirited animal. "Roscoe?"

The chocolate Lab seemed even more elated that she recognized him and increased his barking to a fever pitch, loud enough to echo through the confines of the truck with each jump.

"Roscoe, how did you get out?" She wiped at the tears on her cheeks, her attention moving away from Gavin and to the boisterous animal that had managed to lick those cheeks at least a couple of times in his leaping frenzy.

She leaned away from the dog, even while trying to calm him down. "Come on, boy. Settle down, now. You're obviously feeling better, but you don't need to overdo it."

Gavin said a prayer of thanks, because he suspected God had sent this energized animal to break the tension of that uncomfortable conversation.

"Haley, I'm so sorry!" Breathing hard, Aaliyah, holding one hand to her chest and clutching a bright red leash in the other, appeared from a nearby trail. "I was taking him on his nature walk, and I guess he heard y'all talking. He bolted like he'd seen a snake." She held up the leash. "I must not have had this clipped on completely."

"You think?" Haley asked.

Gavin was thrilled to hear a hint of laughter in her voice, confirming they were moving on from the somberness of a moment ago.

*Thank You, God.*

Aaliyah, laughing, snapped the leash into the D ring on Roscoe's bright red collar. "Okay, boy. Let's head back to the clinic. I still need to walk Honey and Sugar."

"Let's hope they're a little less lively than our best customer here," Haley said, rubbing her hand over Roscoe's head while the dog looked as though he were smiling at her, his tongue lolling out to one side in his happiness.

Aaliyah guided him away from the truck. "Sorry I interrupted your—discussion," she said, giving them a smile and turning away.

She'd barely disappeared down the trail before Haley turned toward him and confided, "I'm afraid the rumor mill may be hopping a bit over her finding us here… *discussing*."

"You think?" he asked, mimicking the tone she'd used to her assistant.

As he'd hoped, she smiled. But then her face sobered. "In case you're wondering, you don't need to worry about me sharing your story. I would never betray your trust that way."

"I believe you," he said, drawn to her honesty and the fact that he *did* trust her with the truth of his past.

"And I can control the rumor mill, in case Aaliyah got the wrong idea. Then again, I'm sure everyone in town knows I'm not interested in a relationship, so we shouldn't have anything to worry about when we're working together on the program."

"You've decided you can work with me now? You aren't going to request a female counselor?"

Her shoulders lifted in a small shrug. "Sorry about that. I would like to work with you, if you still want to work with me."

"I do."

"And I appreciate you sharing your story, more than you could know. I...understand now why you act the way you do."

"How do I act?"

She didn't miss a beat. "Gruff. Grumpy. Irritated."

He fought the urge to laugh. "Don't hold back."

"I might have compared you to a bear," she admitted, and Gavin set his laugh free.

She joined in. "I really am sorry about that. I shouldn't have judged you so quickly."

"I probably deserved it, but why don't we start from now on with me being less grumpy."

"And me being less judgmental?"

He smirked. "I wouldn't have used that word, but if you say so."

"Deal." She extended her hand and Gavin shook it, her petite palm easily fitting within his. The warmth of her hand, the touch from someone who seemed to truly understand him, warmed his heart. Then she grinned, one blond eyebrow lifting as she asked, "So are you suggesting we be friends?"

He hadn't really thought about it that way, but he knew that working together would come a lot easier if they were. However, he hadn't had a female friend since Selah's death, and had only had a very limited number of female acquaintances. So could he? Be friends? With Haley Calhoun?

As if she were reading his thoughts, she asked, "Is the idea of being friends with me that hard to comprehend?" She slid her hand from his shoulder and rested her elbow against the back of the seat.

Gavin found that he missed her touch. Probably not something he wanted to analyze...too much.

"Because if you're afraid I would want more than

friendship, you don't even need to wonder. You know that old saying, 'burn me once, shame on you, burn me twice, shame on me.' I've been burned by men more than twice. And I'm done."

"Who hurt you?" He couldn't imagine anyone intentionally hurting Haley Calhoun.

"Not physically hurt. It's just that every guy I've ever dated ended up deciding I was better friendship material than anything more." She lifted a shoulder as though it wasn't a big deal, but Gavin suspected it was. "In fact, the joke at the Cut and Curl, our local gossip hair salon, is that if a guy wants to settle down and get married, he should date me first." She laughed, but there was no humor in it.

"That…bites."

Her laugh burst free, and he liked the sound of it.

"That's probably the best response I've heard yet, and you're right—it does." She pointed a finger in the air. "So, since it's already been established that I'm friend material, and since you already know I don't want a relationship, I'd say we can count ourselves friends?"

Gavin liked the idea of a friendship without the slightest risk of anything more. "I don't want a relationship again, either."

"Perfect." Her smile claimed her face as she extended her hand again. "Then friends it is."

He took her hand in his, ignored the sensation that seemed to accompany each touch from Haley Calhoun. "Friends it is."

## Chapter Seven

Eli's first visit with Buddy after school yesterday had gone as well as possible, considering the puppy slept the entire time. But Haley had said that was a good sign because it took rest to heal. That was the only communication she'd had with them since she'd had two other patients. A miniature pinscher owned by Daniel Brantley, the youth minister at church, and a snapping turtle owned by Nathan Martin, Mae's oldest grandson.

Since those animals were there to see the doctor, and he and Eli had merely gone to visit Buddy, Aaliyah had taken care of them instead of Haley.

Which was fine.

What wasn't fine, however, was how Gavin found himself *wanting* to glimpse the pretty vet, listening for her voice and smiling when he heard her laughter from one of the exam rooms.

*That* realization had kept him tossing and turning most of the night.

He'd decided that he wouldn't mind having a friend in Haley Calhoun, but he wasn't so certain *friendship* should have him thinking about her that much. Consequently he bristled with restless energy. So when he saw "split firewood" on today's list of discretionary chores, he'd headed to the woodpile.

Most guys would've probably learned this type of outdoor task from their fathers. But Gavin's dad was an English professor at Southern Mississippi, not exactly the camping type. In fact, Brodie had given him his first lesson in cutting firewood three weeks ago, right after he'd arrived at Willow's Haven.

Gavin enjoyed the task immensely, found it a great way to spend time on his own reflecting on the past, pondering the present…and asking God for answers.

Today was no different.

The pile of wood was higher than it'd ever been, and Gavin was grateful. This would take time and energy, and he was ready to expend both. Sharing the truth of his past with Haley yesterday had left him feeling more exposed than he'd felt in a long time. And he still wasn't all that certain how he felt about that.

He placed the first log on the cutting block, positioned it in the center and grabbed the splitting ax. With feet shoulder-width apart, he adjusted his distance from the block so that the blade centered the wood when his arm was fully extended. Then he raised the ax and let gravity and the sharp silver blade do the rest.

It sliced and split the wood, the two pieces falling on either side of the cutting block as the strong scent of fresh-cut pine filled his nostrils. He breathed in deeply, relishing the reminder that *this* was his new life, working each day in a unified effort with other counselors to take care of children God had placed at the home. Chopping wood. Planning devotions. Giving hugs. Teaching the youth in their care that things *can* get better. That though others may have abandoned them, God hadn't, no matter how difficult life seemed.

A noise to his right caused him to turn toward the pile, where a jet-black squirrel sat on top of the farthest log, its full bushy tail flickering as he stared at Gavin. He had never seen a black squirrel, hadn't even realized they existed in any color other than gray. But this one was as dark as night, and fearless, from the look of things.

Gavin wondered what Haley would think of the inky squirrel. Probably wouldn't surprise her at all, its shiny black fur. She could most likely tell Gavin all about the thing. When it came to animals, she knew her stuff.

But she'd still been so nervous on the way to the farm yesterday. And then she'd climbed out, appearing all confident and secure as she headed toward the barn to help with the delivery.

While Gavin knew she was shaking like a leaf inside.

How often did she hide what she was really feeling? And did she share those fears with anyone else, the way she had with Gavin? Had she confided in anyone else about the reason for her discontentment with men in general?

He'd thought about her explanation of why she'd given up on men, that all of her relationships had ended with friendship status. But he suspected there was more to it than that.

Yet she hadn't provided any details.

An hour passed and Gavin continued splitting the logs, his arms burning and mind churning, thinking about the pretty blonde who proclaimed herself his newest friend and who had a problem with men.

And with God.

Mae Martin's words had echoed through Gavin's sleepless night and they again haunted him as he grabbed another huge, heavy log.

*What a shame that such a beautiful young lady who'd been so involved in the congregation seems to have given up on God when she gave up on men.*

Why had she given up on God?

And what was the real reason she'd given up on men?

Because Gavin strongly suspected that one might very well hinge upon the other. And he also suspected that God had put him in Haley Calhoun's path to help her find her way to Him again.

He didn't want to consider the possibility that He might also have intended for Gavin to restore her faith in men.


"Maybe she had a doctor's appointment this morning and has her ringer turned off." Aaliyah performed her usual inventory of the heartworm meds for next week's order of supplies.

Haley entered Buddy's daily progress in his file on her computer but couldn't get her mother off her mind. Obviously, Aaliyah was used to the fact that Haley's mom called every morning and knew this unusual behavior had her concerned, particularly since Haley kept trying to call…and got no answer.

She picked up her phone and tried again. Nothing.

"Even if she had an appointment and turned the ringer off, she'd eventually turn it back on," she said. "And that wouldn't explain why she never called yesterday morning, or why she didn't answer or return my calls last night or today."

"Did your granddad not know where she was or what was going on? He lives with her, doesn't he?"

"He lives in the garage apartment behind her house."

"The apartment you had?" Aaliyah checked the date on another box. "I didn't realize he didn't live in the house with her. That's nice, that he can be near her but still have his independence. Kind of the reason you lived there, right?"

"Yes. I lived there while I was in college." After graduating high school and getting accepted at the University of Florida, she'd been ready to move on campus, but her father had said she could go only if she commuted from home. Haley had been so anxious to become a vet that she would have walked the thirty miles to and from the school each day if that meant she got to go. But, wanting her independence, she'd fixed up the old storage area above the garage.

With her dad's assistance.

Odd, how close they'd been. She'd always suspected that it wasn't a financial issue that had him wanting her to live at home when she went to university. She'd thought the main reason was that he would miss her.

Haley sighed. How different things were then. She'd have never believed the two of them would go a year without speaking. But this month marked thirteen months since he'd announced that, after thirty-eight years of marriage, he'd fallen for a woman he'd met on one of his business trips. Then left her mom on her own to take care of Haley's grandfather.

"Even if he doesn't live in the house, he would see her every day, right? Your grandfather? Did you ask him if he had seen your mom?"

"I *would* ask him, but he also didn't answer his phone yesterday or today. And he isn't great at returning phone calls. He says if someone really wants to talk to you, they'll call back."

Chuckling, Aaliyah logged the heartworm meds on her inventory spreadsheet. "You know, he does have a point. I may stop returning calls, too."

Haley smirked. "That's fine for your personal calls, but I'd appreciate you calling our clients back."

"Gotcha. But it sounds like you should keep calling your grandfather then. Eventually he'll pick up."

"Trust me, I have been."

Aaliyah frowned. "Isn't there a neighbor or a friend you can call to check on her? Or…what about your dad? I mean, he still lives in the area, right?"

"He lives there," Haley said, unable to stop the grimace that accompanied the thought, "but I'm *not* calling him. Especially about Mom."

Aaliyah pointed her pen in the air. "Duly noted. Okay. Maybe someone from her church could check on her?"

"She stopped going to church a year ago." Haley didn't add that they'd both stopped at the same time. "And she doesn't really have anyone that she's all that close to anymore. Most of her time is spent taking care of my grandfather."

"I think it's awesome how she takes care of him like that."

"Yeah, particularly since he's never been the nicest of people. He scared me to death when I was little. Honestly, I never knew how my grandmother put up with him when she was alive." Haley finished updating the files on the computer and glanced at the clock. A quarter to two. "Oh, my. Gavin will be here soon to help me collect the animals for the visit to Willow's Haven."

"*Gavin* will be here soon? Wow. I'm away for a day and he moves to first-name status. The other night, I'm pretty sure I heard you compare him to a bear." Aaliyah's eyes practically glittered with excitement at this new predicament. "And then yesterday, you're sitting at the alcove, in your truck, looking very comfortable with the guy."

"It wasn't anything more than a discussion, trust me."

"I figured, given your stance on men." Aaliyah paused and looked at Haley thoughtfully. "You know, all men aren't like your dad."

"You mean acting like they're committed for life then leaving? The thing is, it wasn't just his leaving that hurt. He knew why I moved so far away, because Doc Sheridan had told me he would be retiring and this was a way to get my own clinic going faster. When I said I wanted to stay closer to home, he encouraged me to move, saying he and my mom wouldn't be at home much anyway once he retired. That they'd be on their own again, like newlyweds."

"That's so sweet."

"Yeah, it would've been. She had been looking forward to that time with him for as long as I can remember. And then, after I've established myself here, not only with the clinic but buying a home, he leaves my mom." She swallowed. "Instead of the retirement he promised, and those trips and great times with my dad, my mom is all alone. And I'm here, five hundred miles away."

"Haley, are you thinking about moving back to Ocala?" Worry filled Aaliyah's tone. She and Haley had gotten close during their time together at the clinic. Plus, Haley knew she liked her job here, even if it was part-time, and who knew whether another vet would let her work the minimum hours she needed to finish her degree and spend time with her little girl?

"I've suggested that to Mom several times, but she keeps reminding me of how difficult it is to start a clinic from the ground up, especially around Ocala, where there's a vet nearly every mile. And she said we can still be as close because we talk every day."

"And then she didn't call."

"Or answer her phone when I called her," Haley lamented. "It's bizarre."

"Maybe things aren't as they seem and everything is A-OK in Florida."

"Maybe so." Haley closed the computer files and viewed the screen saver, a photo of her and her mom from last Christmas. "But if I haven't heard from her by tomorrow, I'm driving down."

Aaliyah noted her place on the inventory sheet and looked pointedly at Haley. "You really are worried about them, aren't you?"

"Yes, I am."

"Well, I'll be praying that you hear from your mom soon."

Haley paused. Gavin had offered to pray for her yesterday. And now Aaliyah.

Everyone kept talking to God on her behalf.

She wondered what He thought of that.

"I'm going to get Buddy ready to go. Can you take Honey and Sugar for their nature walks while we're at Willow's Haven?"

"Sure," Aaliyah said as the door opened and Gavin entered, his sheer presence filling the room like an electrical current.

Or maybe it just seemed that way to Haley.

But…wow.

He wore a navy denim shirt, the sleeves rolled up and consequently showcasing tanned, muscled forearms. Well-worn jeans and hiking boots completed the look of a rugged outdoorsman totally comfortable in his world.

He looked like he'd just come in from hiking. Or riding a horse. Or chopping wood. Building a raft. Or a house. An active man, not afraid of hard work.

He looked like a guy…you'd want to go on a hike with. Or share a picnic. Or ride horses. Maybe go to dinner with.

Build a house with.

*If* you were wanting any of those things.

And she wasn't.

She wanted a friend. Nothing more, nothing less. And, blessedly, that was all he wanted, too.

Which was perfect.

"Oh, look, *Gavin* is here," Aaliyah said, barely above a whisper, but Haley heard and quickly put her thoughts back in order.

"Hey, Gavin. Let me get Buddy and then we can go get the other animals," she said.

"I'll help you." He nodded toward the office as he walked to Haley. "Good to see you, Aaliyah."

"You, too, *Mr. Thomason*," she said.

As Haley led Gavin toward the back, she made a mental note to pinch Aaliyah at the first opportunity.

Gavin stopped to pet Honey and Sugar on his way to Buddy's kennel. "What happened to the other guy— the one that visited us at the truck yesterday? Roscoe, wasn't it?"

"Landon picked him up earlier. They wanted him back at the farm so he can get used to the new filly and so she can get used to him being around."

"Sounds like a good idea."

"It is." She stopped walking to watch him, standing there while Honey proceeded to lick each of his fingers. "I think she likes you."

"What's not to like?" he quipped. When she lifted

her brow, he reminded her, "You forgave me for being a bear, remember?"

"I did," she said. "But that doesn't mean I don't remember how much fun you are when you aren't in the mood for..."

"For what?" he asked.

"For humans."

His deep, rumbling laugh sent a ripple of goose bumps down her arms. She mentally scolded herself for letting her natural response to a good-looking male get in the way of her friends-only status with Gavin Thomason.

Who happened to be a very good-looking male.

If she were saying... Which she wasn't. Especially not to Aaliyah. Or to anyone else in Claremont.

She turned away from Gavin and Honey to find the smallest animal in the place toddling to the front of his kennel and sticking his tiny nose through the gate.

"Well, look at you." She put her finger out for Buddy to lick.

"Yeah, look at him," Gavin remarked. She could tell from the warmth radiating at her side that he now stood directly beside her. "He looks like he's feeling better. And his fur...it actually looks soft."

"The fact that he's got some liquids in him doesn't hurt, and I gave him a bath this morning with a moisturizing pet shampoo that should benefit his skin and coat." She opened the kennel and gently scooped him out.

He continued licking at her fingers and even wagged his tail as she moved him into the crook of her arm.

"You would think he knew he was going to see Eli today," Gavin said.

"I think he can tell something exciting is happening." Haley nuzzled his nose to hers then grabbed the small red leash and collar she'd gotten for the puppy and attempted to put it on one-handed. He kept wriggling free until Gavin, chuckling, slid his hands beneath his belly to hold him still.

"She's just putting your collar on," he said softly. "Stop squirming."

"That's right." Haley snapped the collar in place and checked the silver tag to make sure the clinic's phone number was legible. "I put one of the clinic tags on him for now, but I'm guessing Eli plans to keep him, right? So I'll need to get the Willow's Haven contact information on the collar and then we can update it with Eli's new address after he's placed in a home."

Gavin's mouth dipped to the side. "Brodie and Savvy are doing their best to get approval from the state to keep pets at Willow's Haven, but, so far, they're hitting a wall. The social worker isn't sure it would be beneficial for the kids to get too attached to an animal that might not be going to their permanent homes."

"Why *couldn't* they go to their permanent homes?"

"From what I've heard from Brodie and Savvy, it's because some people are allergic to animals and can't allow them in the home. And some people don't like animals."

She stroked the tiny area between Buddy's ears, gazing down fondly at the puppy Eli already cared so much about. "Well, if you ask me, if the kids get attached to a pet, then they should be able to take that pet with them wherever they go. These kids need all the love they can get. And you can't get any better form of unconditional love than from a pet."

Gavin continued holding the puppy while she secured the leash, standing close enough that he could see the truth of her statement in her eyes. She honestly believed there was no better form of unconditional love?

He'd known God meant for him to support her, so he'd be crazy if he let her statement, or this opportunity, pass him by. "A pet's love is unconditional, but there's also the unconditional love that children should experience from their parents. Some of the Willow's Haven kids haven't known that yet. The ones that were abandoned. Hopefully they will learn about it at Willow's Haven and receive that kind of love in their new homes. But the best example of unconditional love, of course, comes from God."

She took a quick breath, as though she were going to say something, and Gavin wondered if he'd finally get a glimpse into what had caused her to turn her back on her faith. But then she blinked, bit her lower lip and said, "I hope the state will see that the kids could really benefit from having pets of their own. And in the meantime, we'll make sure to give them plenty of opportunities to love these animals."

With Buddy's collar and leash now in place, she slid him from Gavin's palms and held him up to her face. "Isn't that right, Buddy?"

Gavin knew better than to push the subject. Their "friendship" was still fragile, in a very early stage. But he knew with certainty that he was supposed to help her through whatever her spiritual issues were, and he would, eventually.

Right now, however, she wasn't ready for any type of God talk.

"Normally, I'd put a photo of Buddy in the lobby on the Rescue Me wall, but I'm not going to do that this time," she said, forging ahead without giving him any chance of furthering discussions on unconditional love.

"Eli wants him and he should have him. We'll merely wait until that can happen. And in the meantime, we'll make sure they get to spend plenty of time together."

Odd that he didn't find himself recoiling when she'd said "we," naturally including Gavin in her future plans involving Willow's Haven. Without the threat of a relationship beyond friendship, there was no reason he couldn't work wholeheartedly with this incredible, striking lady to provide a great program for the kids.

*Striking*? Where had *that* come from?

Buddy licked her nose and she laughed, her cheeks lifting and drawing attention to vivid green eyes within a bounty of thick lashes. He noticed her blond hair, loosely contained in a high ponytail with wisps curling all around her jaw and down her neck.

He wondered what she looked like with her hair down.

*Whoa*. Okay, so *striking* nailed it. But that was fine. He could have a beautiful, striking friend. He'd had attractive friends in the past, so that shouldn't impact his ability to maintain the friendship status that they both wanted. Plus, he didn't have to look far to remember everything he'd lost when Selah and their baby boy died. Every time he saw a mother and baby, even yesterday when he'd seen the mare and filly, he was reminded of the pain of his past.

And the fact that he didn't want to open his heart up to that potential torture again.

Therefore he needed to get his mind on something other than Haley Calhoun's natural, eye-catching beauty. "Why don't I carry Buddy?"

The tiny dog emitted a high-pitched, excited bark and Haley laughed again.

It didn't help that her laugh was adorable.

"Sure." She grinned as she handed him over. "I would put him in a kennel for traveling, but he's been in this one for a while. I think he'd like to be free, if you don't mind holding him."

"Don't mind at all." He was grateful for the wriggling thing licking at his knuckles, because it kept his mind off his new, extremely attractive *friend*.

"Okay, then, let's go." She moved past him and left him to follow in the wake of apples, cinnamon and a swishing blond ponytail.

No doubt about it. It'd take more than the squirming puppy in his arms to keep his mind off Haley Calhoun.

## *Chapter Eight*

"*This* is your house?" Gavin took a moment to absorb the unique scene. A turquoise cottage with stark white trim accenting the doors, windows and porch. It looked like something belonging on a sandy beach instead of being tucked into the wooded confines at the base of the Lookout Mountains. Exquisite, in a modern yet rustic kind of way. And Gavin liked it immensely. So unique. So distinctive.

So...Haley.

"I may not live in Florida anymore, but that doesn't mean I don't like having those fun beach hues in my world." She grinned as she turned to look at him. She'd left the truck windows down and the breeze played with those blond wisps, several brushing against her delicate cheekbone. "Do you like it?"

"Yes," he said, speaking the truth, whether talking about the house...or the woman who lived there. He absorbed more of the details of her home. A wooden picket fence bordered the perimeter. The vivid red door centering the front porch matched the humongous red barn at the back of the property. "That barn is bigger than the house."

She laughed and nodded. "Which makes sense, since it has more occupants."

Several of the "occupants" came into view as they neared. The most prominent of the lot was a silver horse with a stunning white mane and tail, as well as white hindquarters with charcoal spots. He tilted his proud head and neighed loudly as Haley drove past the house and headed to the barn.

"It's okay, Sterling," she called out the window. "He's a friend." She glanced at Gavin. "Just so you know, he's a bit possessive. Jealous, even."

"Jealous?"

She winked. "You'll see."

And that wink made her even cuter.

*Friends*, Gavin reminded himself. Nothing more. He didn't want anything more, couldn't let anything more happen to his heart.

*God, help us keep this relationship where it needs to be, for both of our sakes. And help me find a way to break through her walls and bring her back to You.*

The other farm occupants came into view as they pulled up to the barn. A fat black cat, perched at the opening to the hayloft, looked mildly perturbed that they had company.

"That's Fang. I'd bring him with us, but he'll only come if he's in the mood to cooperate."

"I'm guessing that isn't typically his nature," Gavin said.

"Hardly, but we'll give it a go."

She parked the truck near the front of the barn and climbed out. "Now, we're only here for a few minutes, but I'll do my best to give you all some attention before we leave," she announced, and Gavin realized she was speaking to the crew at large rather than to him. Then she turned to the other occupant in the truck. "Buddy, you be good in here while we're gone, okay?"

The only one she didn't speak to, Gavin, turned and petted Buddy before also climbing out. Then he stood and grinned, enjoying seeing this part of her "family." Each animal gravitated toward her, even the finicky fat cat that hurled himself from the loft to land near her feet.

"I guess you can see why I named him Fang." She rubbed the cat's back while it made a noise that more resembled an old man's snore than a purr.

Gavin easily spotted the one long tooth hanging out the right side of his mouth in a menacing point. "Fang." He nodded. "Suits him."

Haley continued petting the cat. "I thought so." She indicated an open doorway nearby. "That's the tack room. Fang's pet carrier is to the right inside the door. It's the olive green one. Can you grab it and we'll see if he wants to go visit the kids today?"

"You'll let him decide?" Gavin moved to the tack room to grab the carrier.

"Might as well. If we take him and he doesn't want to be there, the kids won't want him around anyway."

"Good point." He lifted the olive carrier. "How do we know if Fang will do us the honor of joining us?"

"Put it at your feet."

She straightened from the cat and took the lid off a nearby tin garbage can. Reaching her hand inside, she grabbed a fistful of something that looked like corn and tossed it to the side of the barn, where a flurry of hens and chicks he hadn't originally seen suddenly appeared and made a mad dash for the goods.

Haley looked his way to see him standing there, watching her. "Just sit it at your feet," she repeated.

He'd been so absorbed in seeing her in her element
that he had forgotten to follow her instruction. Placing
the carrier on the soft ground at his feet, he watched to
see what the hefty cat would do.

Fang looked at the carrier then at Gavin and then
back at the carrier. If Gavin were guessing what the big
thing was thinking, he'd say he was annoyed.

"Fang, you wanna go for a ride?" Haley asked.

The sizable cat stalked toward the carrier, hissed at
it and then continued his slow stroll toward the back
of the barn.

"You can put the carrier back. Fang has decided he
won't be joining us today. But while you're in there, can
you grab the big gray one? It's in the left corner. We'll
take a couple of rabbits. They won't give us any grief,"
she said with a laugh. "Next time, maybe we'll convince
Fang to come, or we can take some of the chickens."

"You have rabbits?" He easily found the gray carrier. She had the place organized to a T, and he wasn't
surprised. Her clinic had been equally in order, everything labeled and marked and spotless. Obviously she
liked structure in her life.

Or at least in the part of it she could control.

"I have eight rabbits," she said, bringing him back
to the here and now.

He hadn't seen any sign of rabbits yet, but he wasn't
all that surprised she had some. She had a minizoo in
her backyard. "Where are they?"

"Their hutch is on the other side of the barn. I'll
show you, but let me get something for you first." She
walked into the tack room, opened a dorm-size fridge
that sat a short distance inside the door and withdrew
two brown blobs that looked like wet clumps of dirt.

She motioned to the front of the barn. "You can put the carrier over there for a minute while you take these."

He put the carrier where she indicated and then tried to get a better look at the messy things in her hands. "What *are* they?"

"Your peace offerings to Sterling, to prove you aren't a bad person to have around." She walked toward him, and it didn't matter that they stood inside a barn filled with the combined scents of animals and hay and leather, Gavin still caught the distinct smell of apples and cinnamon that surrounded Haley Calhoun.

And made him inhale a little deeper.

"Here." She extended the two blobs toward him.

He took them and she giggled when he grimaced at the gooey texture in his palm. "What am I holding, exactly?"

"Molasses treats. Or 'horse cookies.' You can call them either one. Sorry, they're sticky. If I bought the premade ones, they'd be much drier, but Sterling doesn't like those nearly as much as these. I doubt he'd even eat those now, truth be told." She shrugged. "He might be a little spoiled."

"I'm getting a sense most of your barn occupants are."

She laughed. "Yeah, probably a good assessment."

"Where do you get these?" He followed her around the side of the barn to find the big gray horse sticking his head out to see what was keeping them.

"I make them," she said as though cooking up horse treats was something everyone did.

Gavin wondered if there would ever be a day spent with Haley Calhoun when she didn't surprise him a little. Or a lot. And he had to admit he was beginning to enjoy this new friendship with the interesting lady.

"You *make* horse treats?"

Her laugh echoed against the tin barn. "Don't sound so surprised. It isn't that difficult. Carrots, apples, molasses or honey, oats and vegetable oil. You mix it all up in the food processor, spoon it on a cookie sheet and bake it. Not a big deal, and Sterling loves them." She walked to the horse, which was much larger than he'd seemed when they were in the truck, then stroked her hand down the length of his nose. "Hey, there, big guy. You having a good day?"

The silver stallion nuzzled the side of her head, almost as if he were trying to give her a hug.

"Wow."

Haley turned and grinned. "I know, he's beautiful, isn't he?"

Gavin nodded instead of informing her that the stallion wasn't the only thing beautiful around here. That would *not* be best in keeping to the friendship status they both wanted.

He took a step toward the horse.

The tall animal raised his head from Haley, his long, white lashes lowering as he glared at Gavin and blew an angry puff of air out his nose.

Haley laughed but Gavin stopped moving. He'd never spent *any* time around horses, ever, and he wasn't certain whether that sound was a welcome.

Or a warning.

"Sterling, come on," she said. "He isn't a threat to you. You're still number one in my book."

Odd, Gavin wasn't sure whether he should feel glad she was smoothing his way over with the stallion or insulted that he was playing second fiddle to a horse.

"Go ahead and give him the cookies. One at a time."

Gavin took another step forward.

The horse ducked his head, let out another small puff of air through his nostrils, but seemed to concede, looking at Gavin and showing some interest in the items in his hands.

"Balance a cookie on your palm and hold it in front of him. He'll do the rest," she instructed, her voice soft and easy.

Gavin wasn't sure whether the tone was to calm the horse or him, but he decided now wasn't the best time to ask. Sterling wanted the cookies.

Following her instruction, he placed the first cookie flat on his palm and raised his hand toward the horse's mouth.

Before he had a chance to worry—too much—that Sterling would decide to bite off a few fingers, the stallion's warm velvety lips brushed against his palm and the first cookie was gone.

"He'll want the other one now. One was probably enough, but he saw that you had two, so you'd better give it to him. And pretty quick." A giggle trilled through her words.

Gavin slapped the other treat into his palm and watched as the horse wasted no time gobbling it down. Then he lowered his head near Gavin's arm, nudging him.

"Now you're friends," Haley announced while Gavin took the opportunity to rub his hand down the stallion's muscled neck and marvel at this incredible creation of God.

"He's amazing," he said.

"Yes, he is." She checked her watch. "I think we should start gathering the animals so we won't be late."

"Yeah, the kids get off the bus in thirty minutes."

"That's the good thing about taking rabbits today,"

she said. "They're easy to catch. Grab the gray carrier and follow me. We should get two of them, so each group will have an animal."

She had eight rabbits of varying combinations of gray, white, brown and black in a wood-and-wire hutch spanning nearly the entire length of the barn. Within minutes, they'd easily caught two and had them ready to go in the gray travel kennel settled in the back of her pickup.

"Why rabbits?" He watched the furry balls roll all over each other in the carrier. "I mean, the rest of these come to mind when I think about farm animals. But rabbits?" He shrugged. "Not so much."

"I like rabbits. They're easy to care for. They're cute and, more than that, I couldn't say no to the guy that needed someone to take care of them when he moved away from Claremont." She smiled. "That's the way I got all these animals, except Sterling. You'd be surprised how many show up at your door when you're a vet."

"They're all strays? You rescued all of them?"

"Depends on how you look at it." She closed the tailgate and walked to the driver's side. "I'd say they rescued me. They're my family here, you know."

Once again, Gavin found himself impressed.

And finding it somewhat sad that this was her family now. Then again, he'd lost his own family and now had his own version of an adopted family, with the counselors and kids at Willow's Haven. He and Haley had what they needed now with regard to family, even if it wasn't in the traditional sense.

"One more animal to go. But he stays at the house, so we'll swing by and pick him up."

"Do I need to get another carrier?"

"Nah, he'll ride up front with us." She drove the short distance to the house and then hopped out of the truck. In a flash, she'd jumped the front porch steps and headed inside. He admired her energy, especially now that he knew that, after working all day at the clinic, she returned home to quite a substantial brood to care for. And enjoyed every minute of it.

While Buddy snoozed in Gavin's lap, he kept an eye on the door to see what animal would join them in the cab. He didn't have to wait long to find out. Haley quickly returned with a beagle puppy in her arms.

The dog looked up at her adoringly as she carried him and received an equally affectionate gaze from his owner.

"Need me to hold him?" Gavin asked as she climbed in.

"Oh, no. Bagel has to have his head in my lap or he gets car sick."

"Bagel? You named your beagle... Bagel?"

She shrugged. "I thought it was funny."

"Oh, it is," he said, watching the brown-and-white puppy cross the seat and sniff at Buddy, sleeping in Gavin's lap.

Buddy raised his head, took a much less invasive sniff of Bagel and then went back to sleep. Bagel then turned toward his owner, laid across the center of the seat and plopped his head in her lap.

"*That's* the way he rides in the truck?"

She bobbed her head. "It only took two trips before I figured that out."

"Only," Gavin quipped, deadpan, as he tried not to laugh but failed.

They drove toward Willow's Haven in silence, the autumn breeze drifting through the cab while the dogs in their laps nestled in and slept. For the majority of the short drive, Haley kept her attention on the road ahead and didn't chance a look at her passenger.

But as she turned onto the driveway leading to Willow's Haven, she glanced his way. Sitting there with that strong, masculine profile, breeze blowing against those brown waves, muscles visible despite the loose denim shirt.

And on top of that, a puppy in his lap.

She sure hoped no one at the Cut and Curl got a glimpse of them riding in the truck. They'd naturally assume there was more to this than friendship.

And there wasn't.

There couldn't be. She'd been disappointed enough when every guy she'd dated merely wanted friendship. And then royally disappointed in her father. The type of man she'd thought she was looking for in a husband, but who'd turned out to be the type of man who would trade thirty-eight years of marriage for a female merely two years older than his daughter.

Bagel lifted his head and barked. A bark from the pooch during a drive usually meant his stomach wasn't sitting easy.

"Hang in there." She rubbed his back as the cabins came into view, the Willow's Haven bus easing to a standstill on the opposite side.

"We aren't late," Gavin said, "but we better get ready for those kids quick. They'll get off the bus and make a beeline for us, I'm sure."

"Okay. Let me walk Bagel and make sure he's feeling all right. Then he and I will head to one of the cabins. I'm assuming you'll want to take Buddy to yours for Eli?"

"Definitely."

"Miss Haley! You brought Buddy!" Eli jumped from the last bus step and ran full blast across the area centering the cabins, his pack slapping against his back with every step. By the time he reached her, he was breathing hard and studying the beagle on the end of the blue leash currently sniffing a pile of leaves. "That's not Buddy. Is Buddy okay? I thought you were bringing him today. You said you would." His hazel eyes were filled with worry for the puppy he loved.

"Buddy is fine," she assured him. "This is Bagel. My dog. He's going to visit one of the other cabins while Buddy visits yours. Mr. Gavin has Buddy for you." She pointed to the other side of the truck, where Gavin had climbed out and put Buddy down to sniff around before they headed to his cabin.

"Hey, Bagel." Eli petted him quickly before abandoning them in lieu of the puppy he really wanted to see. "Buddy! Hey! Remember me?"

"Of course, he remembers you," Gavin said. "How could he forget the boy that saved him?"

Eli picked up the puppy and Buddy promptly licked his nose. "You're right, Mr. Gavin. He *does* remember me! Can I take him to see Ryan? Can I?"

"Sure," Gavin said, "but we'll want all the boys to get a chance to hold him, okay? And you still need to be careful with him."

"But he *is* better, isn't he?" Worry crept into his tone. "He's better, right, Miss Haley?"

"Yes, he's better. But he's not completely up to full speed yet, so take extra care when you and your friends hold him. Sound good?"

"Yes, ma'am," Eli said, walking away with Buddy nuzzled in his arms.

"Since you'll have Eli at your cabin, I'll take Bagel to

one of the others, and then we can get a couple of counselors to take a rabbit to each of the final two groups."

"We divided them so that there are two groups of boys and two groups of girls. I thought we could let each of the boy groups have a puppy and each of the girls a rabbit, then next time, we'll swap that up."

He had moved close enough that Bagel leaned toward him to get a better sniff of the man. Haley didn't blame the puppy; she also liked that spicy, outdoorsy scent.

Not that she noticed, that much.

"I think it would be good, for Eli, if we both were together in his group. You know, in case anything happened with Buddy. He has been sick and all, so it would be good to have you nearby, too. And we have plenty of other counselors to take Bagel and the rabbits to the remaining groups."

Mark Laverty, another counselor and a guy Haley knew from when he'd brought his dog to the clinic, had started walking toward them and heard Gavin's comments. "That's a great idea. Jennifer and I will take the other boys' cabin, and I'll get Titus, Isabella, Brodie and Savvy to take the girls' cabins." He looked at the rabbit carrier, grinned. "They're going to love those bunnies."

"I think so, too," Gavin agreed.

"Which means I get this little fellow?" Mark reached for Bagel.

Bagel moved from Haley's arms to Mark's, yipping happily at the guy whose hands must have seemed pretty inviting. He'd already started licking Mark's knuckles. "His name is Bagel," she said.

Mark laughed. "Of course it is." Then he winked at Gavin. "You two have your group covered, right?"

"We do," Gavin said then looked to Haley. "Ready?"

She suddenly realized that this was it. She was starting her first venture on her own as a vet and supporting children who'd been through a rough time. An almost giddy feeling swept over her and she smiled at the man joining her for the effort. "Very ready."

## Chapter Nine

"Why is his nose wet?" Ryan, Eli's best friend in the cabin, asked Haley.

She'd been answering questions from the boys for almost thirty minutes, each boy asking one when it was his turn to hold Buddy.

"Yeah, why is his nose wet?" Eli asked. Even though it was his friend's turn to hold the puppy, he leaned against Ryan and ran his left hand down Buddy's back.

Haley's attention was drawn to that hand and how well he used it despite his joined fingers and gnarled flesh. She was also drawn to the way that neither Ryan nor any of the other boys seemed to notice.

Her heart tugged in her chest. "His nose is wet because dogs need that dampness on their noses to help them smell better. They can use it to absorb a particular scent."

Ryan held Buddy to his neck and the puppy rubbed the wet nose against him. "That's cool," he said. Then, with Gavin's assistance, he gently passed Buddy to the next little boy so he could hold the puppy and ask his question.

"And what's your name?" Haley asked the boy.

"I'm Ben." He had spiked light brown hair, dark-rimmed glasses surrounding blue eyes and a smattering of freckles dusting both cheeks. He bit his lower lip when Gavin started to ease away. "Can you help me hold him, Mr. Gavin? I'm— I don't want to hurt him."

Haley didn't miss the fear in the little boy's eyes, obviously scared he would do something wrong. Her heart tugged again, but this time it was with the realization that all these kids were there because something had gone wrong in their world.

And she wanted, more than anything, to use this program to make their world a little brighter.

"I'll help you, Ben," Gavin said, his voice filled with so much compassion that Haley bit back a sudden urge to cry. Undoubtedly, Gavin knew Ben's story—knew all the stories of the boys in his care—and he knew what to say to help. Like now, encouraging the fearful little boy as he held a puppy.

He would make a great father.

Another wave of sadness washed over her. Gavin *had* been a father, but then he'd lost his wife and son.

And that thought was quickly followed with the question…how had he gone through that—been dealt that heavy blow—and not become angry with God?

"Haley?" Gavin, still huddled around Ben to help him hold Buddy, caught her attention.

She realized she'd zoned out for a minute, hadn't even heard what he'd said. "Oh, I'm sorry." She swallowed. "I missed that."

Gavin looked slightly concerned but murmured, "Ask her again, Ben."

She felt terrible for missing the little boy's question. "Yes, Ben? I'm listening."

"I forgot the question you told me." He looked pitifully at Gavin.

Gavin smiled at him, leaned close to his ear and whispered.

Ben nodded and asked, "Do dogs sweat?"

Gavin's brow lifted, eyes widening as though he, too, wanted the answer. And Haley now understood that he'd been feeding the questions to the boys.

No wonder they'd all been so good.

She gave him a grin, thankful the kids had a man like Gavin Thomason around. They may not have a father, but they had an amazing guy who cared. And he may not have his son, but he had many boys to love.

Her heart warmed and she was grateful that she was here today, seeing Gavin in his element, and being a part of something so meaningful.

"Growing up, I always heard that dogs didn't sweat," she said. "People told me that's the reason they panted."

"Like this?" Eli asked, sticking out his tongue and puffing out air. Which caused all the other boys, even Ben, to give it a try, of course.

Haley laughed, especially when Gavin joined in on the panting. She nodded. "Yes, like that. But a dog's nose can also be wet because he's sweating. And his feet can be wet with sweat, too."

"Okay, guys," Gavin said a few minutes later, easing the puppy from Ryan's arms. "Buddy has been here an hour now, and it looks like he might be getting tired. Everyone got a chance to hold him and ask a question, right?"

They all nodded and a stream of "Yes, sirs" filled the room, followed by several asking when they'd get to see Buddy and Miss Haley again.

Haley smiled at the group. "You'll see me tomorrow.

We're going to the Cutter farm in the morning to visit some animals there. How does that sound?"

Clapping hands, smiling faces and cheers met her question.

"Okay, then." Gavin grinned at their excitement. "What do y'all tell Miss Haley for bringing Buddy here for us today?"

"Thank you, Miss Haley," they yelled in unison.

Then Ben asked, "Miss Haley?"

"Yes, Ben?"

"Um, can we—" he pushed his glasses up on his nose "—can we hug you?"

Gavin watched the play of emotions on Haley's face. She blinked, then her mouth rolled in slightly and she nodded.

"Yes, Ben, that would be great."

The boy scrambled to his feet and wrapped his arms around her.

He was quickly followed by each of the other fifteen kids. All were visibly grateful for the pretty vet who had taken time from her busy day to bring a little joy into theirs in the form of a squirming puppy that, merely a few days ago, had been abandoned and left on his own to try to survive.

Much like many of these boys.

Gavin's chest constricted at the image before him: Haley surrounded by a herd of little boys who couldn't seem to hug her tightly enough or to thank her enough.

The vision sparked thoughts of what might have been.

He'd wanted kids of his own. Several, truth be told. He and Selah had talked often about buying a big farmhouse and filling it up with kids. He'd looked forward to images like that, except, in his plans, the woman had been *his wife*.

The children had been *his children*.

Haley laughed as Eli and Ryan, fighting over who would get the last hug, knocked her backward in their excitement.

Her laugh rippled over him, sent a longing of lost dreams straight to his heart.

And then her eyes connected with his. Her laughter subsiding and head tilting slightly, she mouthed, *You okay?*

They'd only known each other a few days, but she could already read him. Maybe because he'd divulged his past. Or maybe because that's just the way she was, so in tune to the needs of others. In any case, he nodded.

Even though he most certainly wasn't okay.

Haley watched Gavin speaking to the other counselors, discussing how much the kids liked the animals. She listened and took part in the discussion when appropriate, but her mind kept replaying the way he'd looked at her when the boys had hugged her in the cabin.

There had been so much sadness in his eyes, something near anguish on that beautiful, strong face.

But now he'd traded the sadness for a smile. Chatted with the group as though everything was fine.

How often did he have to hide his emotions like that? And did anyone else notice when he was hurting? No doubt he didn't share his pains often. In fact, he surely hadn't wanted to open up about his past with Haley, hadn't planned to, but she hadn't really given him a choice.

She was glad, though. Because instead of thinking he was shutting himself off, being gruff and grizzly, she now understood that he was a man dealing with his heartache the best way he knew how.

She wanted to help him with that, because Gavin Thomason deserved to be happy. Very happy. And the more she learned about him, the more she liked.

"I guess we can load the animals up and take them home now," he said, bringing her back to the present conversation.

"Sounds good," she replied, saying her goodbyes to the rest of the Willow's Haven group before she and Gavin prepared to load the animals into the truck.

Ten minutes later he showed no signs at all of whatever had transpired in the cabin and smiled as he slid the big gray crate filled with sleeping bunnies into the back of the truck. "I think the kids wore the rabbits out."

"The puppies, too," she said, referring to Bagel, sleeping in her arms, and Buddy, already dozing on the passenger seat.

"It was great to see the kids having so much fun with them, wasn't it?" He shut the tailgate and started for the passenger's side.

"Yes, it was, and it reaffirmed my belief that these kids need some animals here full-time to care for, and to love."

He opened the passenger door. "Hopefully, Brodie and Savvy will find a way to get that approved."

"Maybe I could write a letter to the social worker about the benefits of pets in children's lives, how it teaches them to care for others and gives them purpose."

"It certainly wouldn't hurt. And with Willow's Haven being a Christian children's home, you could also include the fact that caring for pets would help the children follow Christ's example of serving."

Haley wondered how he could be so close to God

after the hand he'd been dealt. She certainly hadn't felt that close to Him since her father had abandoned ship. "How do you—" she started, but a neighing horse caused her to stop midsentence.

"What is that?" Gavin peered into the cab, where the sound grew louder.

"Oh, I left my phone in the truck while we were with the kids. I need to get it. It might be my mom." She hurried to the cab, reached over Bagel and grabbed the phone.

Which had stopped neighing.

She stared disbelievingly at the screen while Bagel squirmed into her arms. "It was her, and I missed it!"

Gavin got another glimpse into Haley's world.

A call from her mom took priority.

"Here, I can hold Bagel while you call her back." He reached for the sleepy puppy.

"Yes, please." She gently transferred Bagel to his arms. "Actually, if you wouldn't mind driving, I'll call her while we're on our way back. I'm hoping we get to talk awhile."

"Don't mind at all." He moved to the driver's side, while she darted around the truck and tapped the screen on her phone.

Gavin waited for her to climb in and then situated Bagel the way she'd done on the drive over, his head in Gavin's lap and his body stretched out across the center of the seat. Then he said a quick prayer that he wouldn't be dealing with the effects of a carsick beagle on this trip.

Haley seemed unconcerned with anything but the telephone. She scooped up Buddy, tenderly placed him in her lap and frowned at the phone against her ear. "Come on, Mom. You just called. Pick up."

Bagel stretched out and rolled his head to the side as if he were the happiest beagle on the planet. Gavin grinned, rather enjoying having the pup along for the ride. "He knows what he likes, doesn't he?"

Haley didn't answer. She had the phone pressed against her ear, her free hand pinching the bridge of her nose and her eyes squeezed shut. If he didn't know better, he'd think she might be praying. But given what he did know about her current spiritual status, he suspected that wasn't the case.

"Mom, it's me," she said, presumably receiving her mother's voice mail. "I missed your call, but I'm wanting to talk to you. I've *been* wanting to talk to you. Call me back. It's been two days and I'm worried. Let me know that you're okay. Please."

She disconnected, plopped the phone into the console and let her head fall back on the seat. "We talk every day. *Every* morning. But I haven't been able to get in touch with her for the past two days." Then, before Gavin could ask anything else, she jolted and reached for the phone again. "She doesn't like texting, but since I can't get her to answer, I might as well try, right?"

Gavin nodded. "Right." But he wasn't sure why she seemed so bothered. He did well to talk to his parents every other week, and then it was because he called to check in. They were typically too busy to call and that was fine with him. They knew that if he needed them, he'd call, and vice versa.

But Haley was obviously concerned about missing a daily call from her mom. Or, in this case, two daily calls.

He listened to her tap out a message and then, frustrated, drop the phone back into the console. "Is something wrong with your mom?"

She moved both hands to her face, spread her fingers over her closed eyes and then dragged them down her cheeks before finally answering. "I honestly don't know if anything is wrong or not. If I don't hear from her by tomorrow, I'm going down there and making sure she's okay."

"To Florida?" What had her so worried about a missed call? "Is she sick?"

"I don't know. Maybe? Or maybe not." She shook her head. "I have no way of knowing, since she won't answer the phone and she hasn't called. And my grandfather hasn't called, of course, because he won't do that."

Gavin was usually pretty good at putting two and two together, but in this case, he felt like he was only getting half of the equation. "Your grandfather wouldn't call because…?"

Her head still rested against the seat, but she turned and released a laugh that radiated tension. "Because he doesn't return calls." She held a finger in the air and said in a deep voice, "'If someone really wants to talk to you, they'll…call…back.'" The last three words were emphasized with finger jabs into the air.

Gavin couldn't help but laugh, as well. Even when she was mad, she was cute. "He sounds like a character."

"Oh, he's a character, all right. And one my mother graciously puts up with on a daily basis, bless her heart."

"He lives with your folks?" Gavin appreciated the opportunity to gain a little insight into where Haley came from.

"With my mom," she said. "Or, more accurately, in the apartment behind her house."

Before he could ask the obvious question, she added, "My dad left my mom last year. They're still married, because, bizarrely, she still loves him. But he's living in Orlando now." She closed her eyes. "He left her last year for a woman he met on one of his business trips. She's thirty-two, just two years older than me. So, basically, she could be his daughter." She paused, and Gavin wasn't sure whether he should say something or wait, in case she would share more.

He waited.

After a moment she said, "Mom always went with him when he traveled. She *loved* to travel with him. But then my grandfather got sick and she started staying home to take care of him, because he said he wanted no part of assisted living. She was home taking care of him while dad was…" Her voice quivered. "I don't know why I'm telling you all of this."

Gavin tried to find something positive to say. "Well, I think it's admirable that your mom takes care of her dad."

She laughed, but again, there was no humor in it. "That's the thing. He isn't her dad. He's my dad's father, and he's never even liked her, or been all that nice to her. Or anyone else for that matter. But that's the way Mom is, always taking care of everyone else." She rubbed her hands down her face again. "She needs… someone to care about her."

And now he began to understand how her father had let her down. He'd hurt her mom. And in doing so, hurt Haley, too.

"You obviously care about her," Gavin pointed out as he started down the driveway leading to Claremont Veterinary Services.

"But I'm here, nearly eight hours away."

"She wants you to move back home?"

"No." She shook her head. "The opposite. She's repeatedly told me to stay, even when everything happened last year with my dad, because she said I have this amazing opportunity to have my own practice, to be the sole vet in town. There are tons of vets in Ocala, with all the horse farms around, and I'm the only one here."

"That makes sense," he noted.

"Plus, I bought the house, which is perfect for me. And I have all my animals here. But..." She took a deep breath, pushed it out. "I wouldn't have moved away if I'd have known she'd be on her own."

"She wants your dream to come true."

She snorted. "That's the thing. The veterinary practice wasn't the biggest part of my dream. When I moved here, I had this vision, the same one that she had for me, that by the time I was thirty..." She stopped speaking, turned to him and he could see those green eyes looking...regretful. "Can you just forget I said anything?"

Gavin got another glimpse into the world of Haley Calhoun. "You're fine with me opening up and sharing my past with you, but you want to pick and choose what you tell me?"

She gave him a tiny shrug and squinted. "Pretty much."

"Not a lot to that kind of friendship, if you ask me," he admonished softly. "Besides, you needed to talk and I needed to listen."

"Why is that?"

"So I can learn more about you, Dr. Calhoun, and be a real friend, someone you can count on. And someone you can confide in."

*Someone who cares about you,* he silently added. She'd said that's what she wanted for her mom, but whether she realized it or not, that's what she also needed for herself. He rather liked the idea of being that for her, as long as there wasn't the risk of anything more. And they'd both agreed neither wanted anything beyond friendship. So why couldn't he let himself care about Haley Calhoun?

As a friend. Nothing more, nothing less.

Her phone neighed loudly and she grabbed it from the console.

"Your mom?"

"Yeah, but it's just a text."

"What did she say?"

"'Sorry I didn't catch you. We are traveling and do not have a good signal. Everything is fine. Don't worry about us. Granddad says hello. I will call you Sunday. Love you.'"

"That's good, isn't it? Everything is fine. They're just traveling."

But Haley looked more perplexed than relieved. "Traveling? That makes no sense. She didn't mention plans to go anywhere when we talked earlier this week. And why would she be traveling with my grandfather? He barely leaves the apartment. In fact, he refuses to leave."

"But she said they are fine."

"Yeah, she did." Though Haley didn't sound comforted by her mom's reassurance.

"So…if they're traveling, there probably isn't any reason for you to head to Florida tomorrow, is there?"

Her head still shook, as though she couldn't reconcile the text with the woman who'd sent it. "No, I guess there isn't."

"Good," he said as the beagle in his lap realized they'd stopped moving and raised his head to peer at Gavin.

"Why is that good?" she asked, reaching out to rub Buddy's belly. Unlike Bagel, he didn't care that the truck had stopped moving and merely rolled over and continued sleeping, his tiny mouth open and his pink tongue hanging out to one side.

"It's good because Eli asked if he could come spend some time with you and Buddy tomorrow, after the kids finish their visit to the Cutter farm. I think he was wanting to make sure he got his one-on-one time with Buddy for the day."

She finally released a smile. "I would love for y'all to come see me tomorrow."

"Great. We'll plan to come after lunch and stay until his afternoon soccer game, if that's okay."

"Sounds good, but I'll be at my place instead of the clinic. You can bring him there. I'd planned to bring Buddy home with me this weekend, anyway, since he'll be the only animal here. It'll be easier for me to care for him that way and save me from making a bunch of trips back and forth."

"Honey and Sugar won't be here?"

"Their owners picked them up this morning."

"Okay, then, we'll see you tomorrow," he said, turning off the ignition and climbing out with Bagel in his arms. "Hey, I didn't even think about taking Bagel and the bunnies to your farm before we came back here for my car. Do you want me to take them out there now?"

"I had planned on letting them stay at the clinic until I leave, but if you don't mind, that'd be great. I can keep Buddy, since I still need to get his liquid supplements ready for the weekend, but Bagel likes being at home better than at the clinic. You could just drive my truck, so you don't have to move the animals, and then bring it back here when you're done. You sure you don't mind?"

"No, I don't mind, and this is my current work assignment, assisting you with the Adopt-an-Animal program. So no problem at all."

"Okay, then. That would be great."

"That's what friends are for, right?" he asked, giving her his best don't-worry-I've-got-this grin.

She gave him a full-blown smile and Gavin was happy to have made it happen, especially following her frustrations a few moments ago. "Yes, that's what friends are for. But I really hadn't planned on sharing that much with you earlier. You caught me with my guard down, thanks to my mom's missed call and weird text."

"But that's also what friends are for, being there when you need someone and listening when you need to vent."

"You do realize the danger of that, though, don't you?" she asked, carrying Buddy toward the door to the clinic.

Actually he did, but he said, anyway, "No. Care to enlighten me?"

As if she knew what he was thinking, she gave him a sassy grin, "You might decide you can't live without me." Then she laughed and Gavin laughed, too, not willing to let on that, while she was obviously joking, she'd also tapped in on the truth.

## Chapter Ten

"*What* am I *doing*?" Haley shut the door and leaned against it. Had she honestly sabotaged her own friendship rules in the span of about thirty minutes?

"I'm guessing that question wasn't directed to me?" Aaliyah peered over the lobby counter.

"I might as well have asked him to *marry me*," Haley said, the words escaping like a long groan.

Aaliyah dropped the notebook in her hand, her mouth falling open and her eyes nearly as wide as her mouth. "Okay. I'm all ears. What *did* you do?"

"I told him," Haley said, struggling to recall her exact words, "that getting closer to me was dangerous, because…" She almost couldn't say it.

"Because…?"

"Because he might decide he can't live without me." Haley dropped her head back against the door. It thudded against the hard wood. And hurt a little.

Thinking that was something she deserved, she did it again. And again. Maybe it would knock some sense into her.

While Aaliyah gaped and Buddy barked.

"Wh-what did he say?" Aaliyah asked, clearly enjoying Haley's discomfort way too much for her employment status.

"He didn't *say* anything. He laughed, because I laughed. You know, trying to make light of it. But—" she felt sick "—I'm not so sure I was joking. And I think he knew it. I was more, like, *hoping*." She shook her head. "I so don't want to go there again. And this should be easy, because I know he doesn't want anything beyond friendship. That should keep my thoughts in order, right?"

"Just an observation," Aaliyah said, "but have you *looked* at him? That alone would make it tough for any girl to keep her thoughts in order. And have you seen the way he is around you? Sure, he may say he doesn't want anything beyond friendship, but he likes you, Haley. I mean, like, *really* likes you."

"Aaliyah, he lost a wife *and* a baby, only two years ago. He wants no part of a relationship again. I told him I feel the same way, so if I can stick to that, we'll both be better off." Her head dropped against the door again. "So why did I say that?"

"Maybe because your heart was talking instead of your brain?" Aaliyah quipped. "But that's just a guess."

"A good guess," Haley mumbled. "I've got a chance at a good thing here, a friend that happens to be a guy."

"A very good-looking guy," Aaliyah added.

"Trust me, I don't need to be reminded."

"And a nice guy, too. Look at his job, working with those kids the way he does. And you should see him at church, always taking notes and speaking up with good points during the Bible class. I know I always listen when he speaks," she said. "Then again, I'm pretty sure every female within earshot does." She laughed.

Haley didn't. "Not funny."

"Listen, you've made no secret of the fact that you wanted a husband and babies by the time you were thirty. Then you turned thirty and it hadn't happened."

"If you're trying to make me feel better here, you're doing a pitiful job."

Aaliyah smirked. "Everyone has this ideal plan for their future. Did I plan on getting pregnant at eighteen and being a single mom to a four-year-old at twenty-two? No. But that's my life and I can't imagine it any differently. I love my little girl, and I know that everything will work out for me with a relationship with a guy who will love her, too, in God's time."

Haley knew Aaliyah's story, of course, but she sometimes envied her peace with it. Her assistant trusted in God, not necessarily to give her everything she wanted right now, but to give her what she needed. Haley, on the other hand, hadn't had the faith to continue trusting in Him when she'd had the rug pulled out from under her again and again, with every guy she'd ever cared about, including her own father.

She'd prayed harder than she'd ever prayed in her life when her mother had called her wailing into the phone, saying her heart was shattered, her dreams for the rest of her life up in smoke.

Because he'd lost his head over a girl who was old enough to be Haley's sister.

And he'd done it all after Haley had put her roots down here, thinking that her parents were fine and would be fine together. For many years. They were only in their early sixties. In fact, her mother wasn't even sixty yet. Wouldn't be for another six months.

Haley was certain her mom's dream for when she turned sixty had been somewhat similar to her own dream for when she turned thirty.

To be with the man of her dreams and live happily ever after.

Why hadn't God kept them from getting hurt?

Where had He been when she'd prayed for Him to show her dad what a mistake he was making? Because her mother wanted him back. For some crazy, bizarre reason, she was still head over heels for the man who first won her heart.

Haley closed her eyes. Remembered how much all of that hurt. Remembered why she never wanted to give her heart that completely to any man. She wouldn't let herself be duped like her mom had been.

Not now, not ever.

"But even though your original dream isn't what happened, that doesn't mean that God doesn't have something better in store. Maybe it's with Gavin," Aaliyah continued.

Haley reminded herself of exactly why "just friends" was perfect. "It's not. It can't be. That's the exact opposite of what he wants and of what *I* want," she said. "That dream is gone. I'm content with what I have here and I don't need anything else. We're just friends."

"You sure about that?" Aaliyah asked as the door opened behind Haley and whacked her in the head.

The puppy in her arms yelped when she squeezed him. "Sorry, Buddy," she said, and pivoted to see who had hit her.

Gavin's face was mere inches from hers, so close that she inhaled the outdoorsy scent that reminded her how very masculine he was.

Her breath caught in her throat.

"Hey," he said, "I brought your truck back. Animals are all back at the barn, safe and sound. Well, except Bagel. I put him in the house, which you should lock, by the way. And I gave Sterling another treat. Figured it wouldn't hurt to get in his good graces."

She swallowed. Wished he wasn't being so incredibly kind. "Thanks," she managed to say.

"Hey, you're okay, right? Because if you need to talk…"

She shouldn't have said as much as she already had, and she sure didn't need to talk any more. Not today. Probably not ever. But given she'd be spending a lot more time with him in the foreseeable future, that was a futile expectation. "I'm good."

He looked skeptical but accepted the lie. "Okay, then, I'll see you tomorrow." He looked at her assistant, happily drinking in every word of their conversation. "Good night, Aaliyah."

"Good night, Mr. Thomason," she said. After the door closed, she amended, *"Gavin."* Then she giggled, pointed a finger at Haley and announced, "You are *so not* good."

Gavin didn't know who was more eager to arrive at the Cutter farm, the kids bouncing in their seats on the bus…or him. This time, though he knew seeing the mare and her baby would undoubtedly remind him of his past, he didn't plan to retreat from the beauty of it. Yes, it underscored what he'd lost. But that foal was also an incredible creation of God and he wanted to appreciate the wonder of it.

"Look at that baby horse!" Eli yelled as the barn came into view. "And there's Miss Haley!"

Gavin looked ahead to see the new filly, much less wobbly legged as she neared her mother, the white stripe, or blaze, as Haley had said, down the filly's face shining bright in the morning sun. An incredible image.

But then he spotted the other object of Eli's exclamation. And his breath caught in his throat.

Haley stood near the mare, her white-blond ponytail also shining in the morning sunlight and her face tilted toward the horse's neck as she held her palm toward the mare's mouth. He felt certain she'd probably brought some of her homemade molasses treats for the new mom and, from the look of things, the horse was grateful. Grateful enough to allow Haley to stand right there, beside her and her new foal.

The vision before him of Haley, the mare and the filly, standing in the morning light, took his breath away.

A click sounded from beside him and Mark lowered his phone. "I got that for you," he said. "Sending it to you now."

"Got what?" Gavin asked, his phone buzzing with an incoming message.

"That." He pointed to the photo of Haley, the mare and the filly. "Figured the way you were gawking, you might like a pic. And that way you'll have something to remind you of that pretty vet you're spending so much time with."

"We're working on the program together. And we're *friends*."

Mark smirked, knowing better than to argue. "Anyway, I sent you the pic, in case you want it."

Gavin didn't have time to respond before the bus pulled to a stop and the kids started climbing from their seats. "Okay, guys. Let's stay in our groups and follow instructions from Miss Haley," he directed.

"Yes, sir!" they all yelled, still jockeying for their places in line, all eager to see the horses and spend time at the farm.

Mark led them off the bus and Gavin waited to follow. He hadn't necessarily wanted Mark to take that photo, but he found himself checking his phone to make sure it was still there.

It was. And it was incredible. The beauty of the horses, and the intriguing lady who cared about them, clearly shining through, as though God Himself were drawing attention to the perfection of His creation.

"You coming, Mr. Gavin?" Ben asked, squinting behind his glasses as he started off the bus.

Gavin knew Ben hadn't waited behind because he wasn't eager to see the animals, but more because he wanted to be with Gavin when he did. Ben needed a little more assurance than the other kids. And Gavin knew his story; he'd come from a family with an abusive father. So the fact that he trusted Gavin meant the world to him. "I sure am, Ben," he said gently. "Let's go see that new baby horse."

"Okay." He took Gavin's hand. "And, Mr. Gavin, um, will we *ride* a horse today?"

"I think that's what Miss Haley is planning. They have that round pen over there where she and I can lead y'all on the horses."

He chewed his lower lip. "But they are nice horses, right? And you'll be there to help me?"

The fear in the child was palpable. "I won't leave your side, son," Gavin promised.

Ben nodded and released Gavin's hand when he got to the bus steps. "Hey, Miss Haley," he said as he descended. "Mr. Gavin is going to help me when I ride the horse."

"That's great, Ben." She took his hand and guided him down the last step. "I'm sure you're going to do an amazing job."

Ben continued chewing his lip, but nodded and stepped past Haley. "I'm going to go see the baby first," he told Gavin.

"Good deal. I'm right behind you," he said, looking to the woman who had apparently been waiting on him to exit.

"Hey." She smiled and he was drawn to the fact that she was even prettier when she smiled.

Quite a feat.

"Hey," he said. "The kids are really excited about this morning."

"That's awesome, but I just wanted to check first— how about you? Are you okay? Because I know how seeing Brownie and her baby affected you last time, and if you'd rather not be a part of the farm visits, I'm sure Landon and Georgiana would lend a hand with the kids here. I should've thought of that last night, but it didn't hit me until I got here this morning and saw the horses."

"I appreciate that, but I'm good now. Really. I saw them on the drive in and I only felt…well, awe. It was just beautiful." He looked at her. Her green eyes glistened with excitement for what the day held, blond wisps from her ponytail framed her face and her genuine smile added even more radiance to the incredibly unique woman in front of him.

The mare and baby weren't the only part of that vision that had been beautiful.

"Okay, then let's get started. By the way, they named the filly Blaze."

"Because of her markings?"

"You remembered," she said with a grin. "Yes, because of her markings."

"Great name."

"I know, right?"

He walked beside her to join the kids, all hanging over the fence to view the mare and filly, now with her head tucked under her mother's belly to nurse, which sparked a host of questions Haley answered skillfully. And lovingly.

She really was in her element here.

Next they moved to the round pen, where each child took a turn being led on one of the horses by an adult. Eli requested Haley to lead him and Ben requested Gavin.

"Mr. Gavin, what if I fall off?" Ben asked, his voice wobbling as he neared Bucky, the smallest horse. He was obviously fighting to be brave, even though he was most certainly scared.

"I'm right beside you," Gavin assured him, "and I promise I won't let that happen." He stopped by the horse and squatted to eye level with the petrified boy. "Listen, if you'd rather just watch this time and maybe ride on the next visit, that's totally fine. I'll stay with you."

Ben gazed up at Bucky and then back at Gavin. "I really want to ride today."

"Okay—" Gavin squeezed his shoulder "—then that's what we'll do. You ready?"

Ben's eyes widened as he took another look at the horse, but he jerked his head in a single nod.

Gavin gently lifted him, guided his small foot into the stirrup and then helped him get the other foot in place. "Hold on to that saddle horn right there, okay? And I'll walk you around nice and easy."

Ben gripped the horn as though his life depended on it.

Gavin began walking Bucky, the horse as docile as

a puppy, as though he knew how scared his cargo was. And maybe he did.

Halfway around, Gavin heard an amazing sound.

Ben.

Giggling.

"This—is awesome, Mr. Gavin!" he exclaimed.

Gavin's heart thumped hard in his chest. "Yes, it is," he said, but he wasn't talking merely about the horse. He was talking about the sensation of seeing this precious little boy...happy.

He looked up and saw Haley across the round pen, her eyes fixated on the two of them, and blinking as a tear rolled down her right cheek. *Good job*, she mouthed.

And Gavin agreed. But this was more than *good*. It was *extraordinary*. "Thank you."

She smiled and he wondered if she realized that he wasn't thanking her for the compliment. He was thanking her for this opportunity, because her Adopt-an-Animal program was going to do wonderful things for these kids. It already was. And Gavin was extremely grateful to be part of it.

And to be part of it...with her.

## Chapter Eleven

In the short time Gavin had known the seven-year-old sitting in his passenger seat, he had accurately determined that Eli had only two volumes: loud and louder.

Case in point, they'd barely started down the driveway to Haley's house when he started yelling, "Miss Haley! Miss Haley! Miss Haley!" loud enough for Haley *and* all of her barn's occupants to hear.

Sterling ran to the fence, probably because he thought someone was about to invade the place.

"Eli, I'm sure she heard you," he said.

"She did!" he said happily. "Look, she's waving! Hey, what's that she's working on?"

Gavin looked up to see her pulling on something to the left of the barn. "That's the rabbit hutch. It holds the rabbits that we brought to Willow's Haven yesterday," he said, but he couldn't tell what she was doing to it.

"Is that, like, their home? That's where rabbits live?"

"It's where those rabbits live," Gavin answered. "But those are tame rabbits. Some rabbits live in the wild."

"In the wild?" Eli asked. "What does that mean?"

"It means they don't live in pens or cages. They live outdoors, in the woods." He knew Haley could do a much better job explaining this and should have waited for Eli to ask the expert.

"Like, in trees?"

"In burrows. Kind of like tunnels in the ground where they make their home and stay safe from storms and other animals."

Eli nodded and Gavin figured it wasn't a bad description, given he wasn't a vet and wasn't a hundred percent certain whether rabbits didn't live in trees, or at least in the hollow stump portion. He made a mental note to ask Haley about that later. And he made a second mental note to always direct Eli to the vet for his animal questions.

"Uh-oh," Eli said, "I think she hurt herself!"

Gavin saw the same thing. Haley, pulling on a wire and then dropping it as she grabbed her right hand with her left, her face wincing in pain. He quickly parked the car and got out, Eli following closely at his heels. "What happened?"

"Are you okay, Miss Haley?" Eli asked from behind him.

"I—think I am, sweetie," she said, but Gavin saw the trail of blood sliding across the top of her hand, her face draining of color. He prayed she didn't pass out before he could get her bandaged. Or taken to Claremont Hospital for stitches, if necessary.

"How bad is it?" he asked quickly.

"I think it looks worse than it is, or I hope it does." She looked like she was going to hurl. "I was tightening the wire where it'd gotten loose. I should've put on some gloves, or used pliers. But I thought I would be okay to pull it with my hands. It sliced the skin between my thumb and first finger." Her breath came out in a whoosh and then she sucked in a gulp of air that made

Gavin think she wouldn't remain standing long. "Amazing how much a little cut like that will bleed, huh?"

Gavin took in every detail, but it was hard to tell how deep the cut was because of the blood. It dripped to the ground at her feet, and she looked toward the sky to keep from seeing it, which probably wasn't a good idea, since she wobbled where she stood.

"Oh, no, Buddy, don't do that!" Eli yelled, and Gavin saw the little puppy heading toward the bloody droplets.

"Eli, you get him while I tend to Miss Haley. You can take him over there in the grass to play, okay?"

"Yes, sir." He carefully scooped up the wiggling puppy before Buddy made it to the red blob on the ground. "Is Miss Haley gonna be okay?"

"I'm going to be—fine," she said, forcing the words out and wobbling again.

Gavin wrapped an arm around her to keep her steady. "Where's your first-aid kit?" He tried to ignore the initial awareness that this was the first time he'd had his arm around a woman in two years. And that this was his first time to have his arm around Haley.

"Tack room."

"Okay, let's get you there." He guided her into the barn and to the tack room.

"I'm so embarrassed," she whispered while he grabbed a wooden chair and set her on it. "I'm around blood all the time with the animals at work, and I have no problem bandaging other people's cuts and scrapes."

"But it's different when it's your own?" He spotted the first-aid kit and grabbed it from a nearby shelf.

"Very different," she said with a shaky grin.

He was thankful for that grin, and for the fact that the color was returning to her face. "All right, let's see what we've got."

She slid her left hand away and looked toward the open doorway, away from the blood that covered the majority of her right thumb and forefinger. "How bad is it?"

He took an antiseptic wipe and cleaned the blood away, then took another to clean the actual cut. "Amazing there was that much blood," he said.

Squinting, she turned her head slowly to view the damage. And her laugh burst free. "That's *it*? It—it's not even a half inch." She shook her head. "Okay, now I'm *really* embarrassed."

Gavin took a small bandage, put a dab of antibiotic ointment in the center and then covered the cut. "Well, what it was lacking in size, it made up for in volume… of blood." He tried to keep his tone serious. But then he looked up at her and saw those green eyes practically dancing.

"Go on," she said, punching him with her free hand, "admit it. I'm pathetic."

"Only when it comes to your own blood loss," he clarified. "You know, though, in all seriousness, you shouldn't work on things like that when you're the only one here. What if the cut had been worse?"

"I'm pretty sure I would've toughened up and done something about it before I risked bleeding out." Her laugh turned into a chuckle.

But Gavin wasn't laughing. He took a couple pieces of white adhesive tape and secured the bandage in place, then looked up at his new friend. The one he hadn't been able to completely get off his mind since she'd showed him a glimpse of her own pain yesterday. "Next time you're wanting to work on something around the farm, I want you to call me. You shouldn't be doing things like this alone."

"How do you think I've gotten everything done so

far?" She quirked one arched eyebrow along with one side of her mouth.

Gavin knew she wanted to be independent, and he admired her for it, but she also needed to be smart. And he didn't like the thought of her here, alone, bleeding, or hurting, or anything that might involve discomfort. "I don't doubt that you did everything here on your own, but there's no reason to do that anymore," he said gruffly. "So call me. Please."

She blinked, finally understanding that he wasn't joking around. In fact, she didn't even want to think of how long her hand would've bled if he and Eli hadn't arrived when they did. True, the cut was small, but she couldn't tell that, and she was so queasy that she might have actually passed out before she'd gotten to the tack room.

"Okay," she said softly, "I'll call."

"I'll hold you to that." He closed the lid on the kit then put it back in its place on the shelf.

He acknowledged that he didn't feel awkward, being here with Haley, taking care of her, even having his arm around her. He liked being with her. But he knew their friendship would take careful handling, to keep their feelings from going down the wrong path.

Especially if he continued to get closer to her.

Which meant he probably shouldn't try to get her to open up more about the conversation she'd started yesterday.

Yet he couldn't resist.

"Haley, you said something about your vision for when you turned thirty."

She stood from the chair and started toward the doorway leading out of the tack room. "And I also asked you to forget I said that," she said over her shoulder.

"I want to be there for you."

She stepped out of the tack room and smiled. "If you're wanting to help me, I can tell you how. And maybe Eli might want to pitch in, as well." She cupped her bandaged hand around her mouth and yelled, "Eli, would you like to help me paint my fence today?"

She ignored looking at Gavin, probably because she knew she'd see his disappointment at her dodging his question.

Eli scooped up Buddy and scrambled to his feet. "Sure! Can Buddy help, too?"

"Buddy can hang out nearby, but we don't want to let him around the paint. Okay? It would make him sick if he accidentally ate some of it."

"Okay, Miss Haley!"

After a beat, she turned to Gavin and asked, "Will you help me, too?"

"Of course," he said, but he planned to help her with more than painting a picket fence. He also planned to help her find her way back to happiness, and to hope… and to God.

"I'm not very good at painting," Eli said, his tongue sticking out the side of his mouth and his brow furrowed as he moved the brush up and down his current picket.

Haley hardly noticed the injuries to his hands anymore. She simply looked at him and saw Eli, the little boy who touched her heart. But she should have considered the difficulty he might face with the task. However, he had almost finished the section of fence he'd selected and he hadn't complained at all.

"You're doing a great job, Eli. And I'm so very happy that you're helping me. Doesn't this fence look better painted white instead of that plain old wood?"

"But I keep missing some spots, and it's kind of tough to hold on to the brush for too long." He wasn't crying, but he looked like he could pretty easily.

She, Gavin and Eli were each working on their own section, and she noticed Gavin had stopped painting and was instead looking at the little boy working in the section between them. He visibly swallowed, and Haley took that as a sign that he didn't know what to say, or was too affected by Eli's dilemma to say anything at all.

Eli had lost his family, and so had Gavin. No wonder Gavin seemed to have such a personal relationship with the little boy. And no wonder he seemed to be having a difficult time figuring out what to say when Eli's scarred hands served as a permanent reminder of everything he'd lost.

Haley wanted to hug both of them, but that wasn't what Eli needed right now. He needed encouragement. So she scooted toward him and petted Buddy, who had moved alongside the boy as he'd worked his way down the section. "I miss spots, too," she said quietly.

"You do?" Eli leaned back to take a better look at Haley's pickets.

"Sure I do," she said, "because it's tough to see the areas you've missed until the paint dries out. But I tell you what—I'll go behind you and get any spots I see that you missed, but you have to promise to get any spots that I miss when you see them, too." She held out her hand. "What do you say? Deal?"

His face relaxed, mouth eased into a smile, and he shook her hand. "Deal."

She petted Buddy again. "And you're doing a great job watching Buddy, too. He hasn't gotten near the paint."

"He does good if I talk to him and tell him what I'm doing."

Haley grinned. She and Gavin had been listening to him talk—even sing—to the puppy throughout the morning. "I think you're right." In fact, Buddy wagged his tail each time Eli spoke, whether he was talking to the puppy or not. "This little guy really likes you."

"He loves me," Eli corrected.

"Of course he does," Gavin said, obviously pleased with the way Eli's disposition had lightened. And, from the way he looked at Haley now, he was also pleased with the way she'd handled Eli's frustrations.

He caught her gaze, mouthed, *Good job*, in the same manner she'd mouthed the same message to him with Ben this morning.

She smiled, happy to have bolstered the spirits of the boy they both cared so much about.

Bagel barked from the front porch, probably because she was still petting Buddy. Her pampered beagle had been watching and barking all afternoon, but hadn't bothered venturing from his favorite spot to see what they were working on.

"He's kind of lazy, isn't he?" Eli asked, and Haley heard Gavin's muffled laugh.

"This is Bagel's day off," she said.

Gavin released his laugh completely. "His day off? What does he do on his day *on*?"

"Hey, watch it. You'll hurt his feelings," she warned.

But Gavin kept laughing. And she joined in. Eli, too, giggling while he moved to the next picket and slapped the paint on the middle.

Haley also proceeded to the next picket in her path and purposely left a few spots uncoated. Then she waited a beat and said, "Eli, just let me know if you see any spots on mine, okay?"

"Yes, ma'am." He leaned back and peeked toward her section. "Miss Haley, I see a few."

"Really?" she asked. "Can you fix them for me? And I'll check yours for you."

"Okay, I will." He moved to her picket, and she swapped places with him to catch the missing areas on his.

Gavin had moved to another picket of his own, but he hadn't missed the conversation, obviously, because he said, "Hey, Eli, when you finish checking Miss Haley's, can you come look mine over for spots?"

"Yes, sir," Eli said, still painting the small patches devoid of paint on Haley's picket. Then he moved to Gavin's and pointed to the middle. "I see one there, Mr. Gavin. Do you want me to fix yours, too?"

"Sure, Eli. That'd be great," he said, moving on to another picket.

Haley had shifted to the next section, but glanced to the guy who, with each passing day, was meaning more and more to her. He grinned at her, and she noticed that he'd at some point wiped his cheek with white paint.

"You have a little paint," she said, "right here." She meant to touch her cheek with her finger, but she had a paintbrush in her hand, so she inadvertently slapped paint on her own cheek.

He laughed. "What do you know? You have paint right there, too."

Eli looked at both of them, then took his own paintbrush to swipe at his cheek. "Now we're all the same!"

"How about that, I guess we are." She couldn't control her smile, or the happiness at being there, with both of them, painting a picket fence and enjoying the day together. She couldn't remember the last time she'd had this much fun, or felt like life might actually be *right*.

She blinked, her throat tightening at the awareness that this, right here, right now, looked extremely similar to her dream.

A car horn sounded and they all turned to see a black pickup coming up the driveway.

"Hey, there's Mr. Mark!" Eli yelled.

Mark pulled his truck parallel to the fence and scanned the scene before him, putting his hand to shield his eyes from the afternoon sun while he gazed at the house and the barn. "Wow, you've really changed things up out here, Dr. Calhoun. I remember when Zeb Shackelford had this place. It was pretty much an old shack, but you've got it looking brand-new."

"Thanks."

He looked at the three of them and tilted his head. "But it looks like y'all are getting as much paint on yourselves as the fence."

Eli laughed. "We were painting ourselves so we would all look the same. 'Cause we like each other."

Haley's throat tightened even more. She had accidentally painted her cheek, and Gavin's swipe at his had definitely been an accident. But Eli's had been undeniably intentional.

Because he wanted to be like them.

Gavin cleared his throat and she suspected he'd been as touched as she was by the little boy's statement.

"You definitely all look alike," Mark said, grinning, "so mission accomplished." He pointed to Eli. "But are you ready for your soccer game?"

"Is it four o'clock already?" Gavin withdrew his phone from his pocket and checked the time. "Oh, I see I missed your texts. Sorry about that. Let me clean up my stuff here, and we'll be right there."

Mark shook his head. "Savvy said she thought you and Eli were probably helping Doc Calhoun here, so she asked me to swing by and pick him up for the game. We've got plenty of coaches, so you don't need to worry about coming. You help finish this fence. And try to get some paint on the pickets while you're at it."

Gavin nodded. "Okay, then, and I will."

"Can Buddy come watch me play, Miss Haley? I almost made a goal at the last game. Maybe he could see me score."

"Probably need to leave him here this time, Eli, but I'll try to bring him to another game, okay?"

"*You'll* come see me play, too?" he asked excitedly.

"Yes, I would love to see you play."

He was still on the ground near the last picket he'd painted and he crawled on his hands and knees, with Buddy toddling nearby, to Haley. Then he wrapped his arms around her and squeezed. "Thank you, Miss Haley."

She nodded. That was all she could do without letting tears fall. This little boy was latching onto her heart, big time, and he didn't even realize it.

Then he stood and told the puppy, "You stay here and be good for Miss Haley, okay?"

Haley blinked. "He will be. And you have fun at soccer."

"I will!" He moved toward Gavin, already getting to his feet.

"Let's get your soccer uniform from my car, so you can go with Mr. Mark," he said, but his voice sounded thick, as though he had sensed the same kind of closeness between the three of them that she'd felt.

Very similar to how she suspected a family of her own would feel.

She swallowed past the dream of the past and watched Gavin and Eli walk toward the barn, where his vehicle was still parked, and was amazed at how they looked together, the tall man and the little boy beside him, chatting as they made their way to the car.

Haley grinned at the two of them.

"He's a good guy," Mark said from behind her, reminding her that she wasn't alone.

She turned to see his arm resting on the open window. "Yes, he is."

"If you ask me, the two of you would be good for each other." He gave Eli a thumbs-up when he held up his soccer gear and started running back to them.

"Oh, no, it's not like that. We're just friends. Neither of us wants anything more than that, but I'm glad to be a friend for him."

Mark smirked. "You sound like Gavin." He lifted a shoulder. "I'm just saying that he could use someone in his life to care about." He studied her for a moment and then added, "Most people could."

"I'm ready!" Eli yelled, his breath coming in gasps as he neared the truck.

"Make sure you save some of that energy for the game," Mark said, grinning. And then to Gavin, walking back to the place he'd been painting, he said, "And we've got everything covered with the kids. So don't worry about a thing." He held up a finger. "That's a directive from Brodie and Savvy, by the way."

Gavin nodded. "Got it."

Mark drove away with Eli waving from the back seat. And Haley was left alone with Gavin, half a wooden picket fence left to paint and Mark's words about Gavin needing someone in his life to care about echoing through her thoughts like a mantra with every pass of the paintbrush over the wood.

Gavin poured the rest of the paint into his metal tray and headed to the last wooden section of fence. "Looks like we're going to have just enough to cover it all."

"That's great." Haley finished her current section and moved to help him with the last one. "We should be able to finish this in nothing flat." She smiled and he returned the gesture, finding it interesting that he was so comfortable here, painting a fence, with Haley Calhoun.

He had a strong feeling that Brodie, Savvy and probably even Mark had set this up intentionally, the two of them at the farm working together while Eli and the other boys were at the soccer game. Mark had been hinting, not so subtly, that it was time for Gavin to move on to another relationship. Brodie and Savvy had told him repeatedly how happy they were that he and Haley were running the Adopt-an-Animal program.

Which wouldn't be that odd, except that Savvy seemed way too excited every time the two of them were mentioned in the same sentence.

But Gavin wasn't complaining. He liked being here, with Haley, even if he didn't want the type of relationship they all had in mind.

He'd *had* the love of his life, and he didn't want, or need, to give that much of himself again. He didn't want to betray what he had with Selah or risk going through that kind of pain again, if he fell completely in love with someone…and then lost that part of his heart.

"Oh, hey, where did you come from?" she asked.

Gavin's attention jerked away from the memories

of the past to the woman beside him who was jumping toward a gray squirrel, scurrying away with her thin paintbrush in his mouth. "Wait a minute, don't take that!" she shrieked.

Buddy barked and Bagel howled. But nothing stopped the furry thing, scampering away from the yard and toward the wooded area nearby, with Haley chasing after him.

Gavin knew there was no way they could catch him, so he picked up Buddy to keep him from playing in the paint and watched Haley do her best sprint across the yard and into the edge of the woods. Then she turned around, put her hands on her thighs and caught her breath…while Gavin laughed.

She wagged a finger at him. "I thought you were my friend."

"I am."

"Then why aren't you running beside me?"

"So both of us can acknowledge we can't catch a squirrel? Then who would keep Buddy out of the paint?" He held up the tiny brown-and-black pup and grinned when she shook her head on her walk back.

"That was the only trim brush I have," she said, breathless from her run.

"We'll be fine with the bigger ones." He gave Buddy a chew toy Haley had brought out of the house. "You're pretty quick, by the way. Did you run track?"

She pointed a finger in the air. "Last leg of the four-by-four relay."

"Wow," he said, impressed. "So you were the fastest on the team, huh?"

She laughed. "Hardly. I was fast enough to be on the team, but lousy at passing the baton. They put me at the end and counted on the fast ones getting us far enough ahead that I could still hold my own."

He was shocked at her honesty but found it adorable. "That's hysterical."

"Yeah, well, it's the truth. How about you? Ever run track?"

"Last leg of the four-by-four," he said, pointing a finger in the air to match her previous pose.

"Because you dropped the baton?"

"Nah. I really was the fastest on the team."

She laughed. "Which means you probably could've caught that squirrel!" She nudged him as she plopped down beside him. "What am I supposed to do the next time I paint and need a trim brush?" She grabbed the other big brush and frowned at it.

Gavin returned her nudge with his shoulder. "I guess we'll just have to buy you another one before our next painting expedition."

"You're offering to help me every time I paint around here? I haven't even started the back deck yet, and there are still two rooms in the house to be done."

"I told you to call me whenever you were working, and I meant it."

"In case I cut myself?" She dipped the brush in the paint and started on one of the remaining pickets. "Hardly any way I can hurt myself painting."

"You said you'd call and I said I'd help."

"You always this stubborn?" she muttered, her brush pausing on the picket while she awaited his answer.

"Maybe," he said, and she smirked at him, her hair, as usual, falling haphazardly from her high ponytail, and her green eyes squinting in the afternoon sun. Add the smear of white paint on her cheek and she looked…

He struggled to find the right word and then settled on...*perfect*.

He wanted this friendship to work, but keeping his mind focused on maintaining status quo was going to be a challenge to say the least.

But that's what he wanted, what they both wanted.

And he was glad for that. Wasn't he?

She moistened her lips and he realized they'd both stopped talking. And were merely...staring. Or gazing. Or something that suddenly made him uncomfortable.

Apparently she sensed the same thing, because she turned and peered into the woods, where the squirrel—and her paintbrush—had disappeared. "Sneaky little thing. We have tons of squirrels around here, of course, but I don't think I've ever had one that stole something from me. And in broad daylight, no less." She huffed out a breath and grabbed her paintbrush.

He welcomed the change in subject. It reminded him of the squirrel he'd seen the other day on the woodpile. "I hadn't realized they'd get that close to people, until I had a black one actually come sit beside me when I was chopping wood."

She'd started painting the last picket, but stopped. "You mean dark gray? Or actually black?"

"Not gray at all. Jet-black. I'd never seen a black one before, didn't even realize they came in that color."

"When did you see it? And what state were you in? I know there are some around the DC area, but even when I went there, I didn't see one. I did a study on them when I was in vet school. They're so interesting." She leaned forward, all thoughts of painting the fence forgotten.

Gavin had known the animal was unique, but he certainly hadn't understood *how* unique. "You haven't seen one? I saw this one at Willow's Haven, earlier this week."

She shook her head. "That couldn't—they're not in this part of the country. Not yet."

Since she'd stopped painting, he reached in front of her with his brush and worked on the last picket. "Trust me, this one was there."

"Jet-black? The entire squirrel, right? Darker than night?"

Her interest made him wish he'd at least attempted to snap a picture with his phone. "Shiny black, I'd say." He dabbed at the final spot on the fence.

"Wow, I would love to see it. A genetic mutation causes that blacker-than-black fur. In the gray squirrels, their color is actually composed of black, orange and white stripes. But in black squirrels, the pigment gene is switched off, so that there isn't any orange and white. And you only get the black."

He enjoyed seeing her face light up when she spoke about animals.

"He was beautiful, wasn't he? The squirrel?" She leaned toward him, enough that he could see the tiniest of freckles sprinkled across her nose.

*She* was beautiful.

"Could've been a girl," Gavin pointed out, hopefully not letting on to where his thoughts had headed.

"Good point," Haley acknowledged with a laugh. "It's just so unreal. I've never heard of any sightings in Alabama…and you saw one right here, in Claremont."

To keep himself from staring at her, since she was so incredibly cute when she was excited, he began gathering the paint trays and brushes. "Yep, I saw one here. Guess that means I'm special, huh?"

Unfortunately the last paintbrush didn't make it completely into the tray and tilted on the edge. Gavin tried to catch it, but only managed to hit the end and cause it to spin…spraying paint all over her face.

She pointed her paintbrush at him. "Oh, you're special all right." Taking her brush, she reached for the top tray in his hand and dipped the end in the remaining paint.

"Haley," he growled in protest, "you know that was an accident."

She nodded slowly. "Of course, I do." And then she flicked her wrist, sent a white spray of paint across his face…and took off running.

Gavin dropped the trays on the ground, grabbed his brush and accepted the challenge.

Haley darted around the back of the house as fast as her legs would go, but she knew the tall, muscular man who just happened to be the fastest on his track team would catch her…so she dove behind an oversize azalea bush at the side corner and waited.

Sure enough, Gavin passed by.

She held her hand over her mouth to keep from giggling aloud. And was supremely shocked at what she was doing. Not the fact that she'd sprayed him with paint, but the fact that she was flirting.

Plain and simple. No doubt about it. And she shouldn't be. It made no sense.

This was strictly friendship. And it would stay there. She remembered her own parents goofing off, flirting, having fun as a couple in front of her, giving her a glimpse of what she could look forward to in a mate. Look forward to in a marriage.

Then she'd seen what else could happen. More heartache than anyone deserved. And she didn't want that.

So this would stay where it should be. Friendship zone only. Even if whatever they were doing right now seemed to border on crossing that line from friendship into flirtation.

But friends could chase each other around with paint-brushes, too, she supposed. And she sure was having fun. More fun than she'd had in quite a while.

She left the bush and prepared to catch him off guard when he circled the house again. But a noise caught her attention. A croak. A very loud croak.

And she remembered today's ringtone.

Bullfrog.

She didn't want to risk missing a call from her mother, and with no sign of Gavin in sight, she jogged toward where she'd left her phone on the front porch.

He jumped out and grabbed her right before she reached the porch, took his paintbrush and touched it to the tip of her nose. "Payback," he said.

Haley couldn't think. Definitely couldn't speak. She was in his arms and he was looking down at her, smiling, with the paintbrush in his hand and mischievous-ness in those bright blue eyes.

And she could only think…*we're supposed to be just friends*.

The croaking had stopped but then started back up again, and Gavin eased his hold on her as he looked toward the sound. "What *is* that?"

She swallowed, wondering if he had felt anything as he'd held her in his arms, right here, next to his chest, so close that she was pretty sure she felt his heart beating. "It's—my phone." She reluctantly wiggled free from his embrace. "I need to get that, in case it's my mom."

Hurrying to the porch, she grabbed her cell and was

shocked at the name displayed on the screen. She answered, "Granddaddy?"

"No, this isn't your granddaddy, dear, but he's right here. Hang on a sec."

Haley didn't recognize the voice and she looked to Gavin, walking toward the porch, his paintbrush still in hand. "It's a lady…on my grandfather's phone," she whispered.

"Is he okay?" He scooped up Buddy, since he'd wandered toward them to see what the commotion was about. Then he sat beside her on the porch.

"I think so." Haley listened to the woman on the other end.

"Henry, it's your granddaughter."

"You called my granddaughter? On my phone?"

Definitely his voice now and he was ticked.

"Granddaddy?" Haley said, but he was still talking to the other woman.

"Ivalene, you are pushing my buttons," he said gruffly. "I told you, I don't call people back."

"You had eleven missed calls from her, Henry. You're being rude, and you need to let her know you're okay."

Haley listened as they continued to fuss and then, finally, she heard, "Hello?"

"Granddaddy? Hey, how are you? I've been calling," she said, as if he didn't know. "Um, where are you?"

"I'm at Shady Palms. Your mom was going to tell you all about it when she gets done with this trip, but Ivalene had to be all impatient."

Haley heard Ivalene scolding him again for not calling her back. But her grandfather merely grumbled something at the lady and then returned to his conversation with Haley.

"I was getting bored sitting in that apartment all the

time. I saw a commercial for this place and I asked your mom, you know, if I could come check it out while she went on one of those trips she's been wanting to take. You know I don't like taking trips. Never liked sitting in a car for more than an hour, and I never trusted planes. So I came for a visit a couple of weeks ago and decided they needed me here."

"*Needed* you here? Of all the arrogant…" Ivalene continued, on a tirade, and Haley actually heard her grandfather laugh.

*Laugh.* She wasn't certain she'd *ever* heard him laugh.

"You—like it there?"

"Ah, it'll do," he said, which must have irritated Ivalene even more because she started listing all of the other places he could go live and asking if he needed directions.

Which earned more low chuckles from her grandfather.

"Granddaddy," Haley said, baffled by the change in the man she'd always known to be a grouch, "what trip is Momma taking?"

"Right now, she's in Branson, I think."

"Branson? As in, Missouri?"

"Only Branson I know." He again released a small laugh.

Who was this man and what had he done with her grumpy grandfather?

"I don't understand." Clearly an understatement. "Mom has started traveling, and you decided to move to an assisted-living center. And all of this happened in the past two weeks?"

"Well, ever since she and—" He paused, waited a

couple of beats and then asked, "She hasn't talked to you lately?"

"Not in the past few days, and she hadn't mentioned anything about a trip to Branson. Or anywhere else. And you never said anything about moving to an assisted-living center," Haley said. "Is she okay? Are you? What's going on?"

Beyond Ivalene, still fussing in the background, silence echoed through the line.

"Granddaddy?"

"I'll tell you this. She's a whole different person with that new church group she's got, and I'm glad for her. She's been mighty sad over the past year. With good reason, you know. Don't know what got into my boy hurting someone as good as your momma, but, well, everything's gonna be okay now. She didn't tell you about the church yet? Or…anything else?"

"N-no, she hasn't." Haley's head was spinning at the overload of information. Her grandfather *complimented* her mother. He'd also admitted that her dad was in the wrong. Another first. And her mom had started traveling—on her own? More than that, she was going back to church?

The last time they'd discussed religion, her mother—and Haley—had agreed that God hadn't done them any favors.

What…had…happened?

"Haley, they just announced that bingo will be starting in a moment, and if I don't get in there, Ivalene will start cheating and win all the good prizes."

Ivalene hadn't stopped disputing practically everything he said throughout the conversation, and that didn't let up now. Which seemed to thrill her grandfather.

"I'll talk to you later, Haley. Call me when you want to talk. You know I don't call back."

The last thing Haley heard before he disconnected was Ivalene's reprimand for that parting remark and her grandfather's deep, rumbling laugh.

She looked at the phone in disbelief. Then glanced up to see that Gavin had left the porch and cleaned up all the paint supplies, stacking the trays and balancing the brushes inside.

He walked toward her now, all of it stacked in his arms, and placed the stuff on the ground by the porch steps.

"I thought you might want some privacy for the conversation and Buddy seemed thirsty so I took him for a drink." He pointed behind her and she turned to see Buddy, all four paws drenched as he stood inside Bagel's water dish to get a drink. "He was too little to drink it over the edge."

Haley was happy for the sweet diversion from the awkward phone call. "I have a smaller dish inside for him, but that's fine."

"So…how's your grandfather?"

"He seemed…" She thought about the way he sounded and all that unexpected laughter. "Better than ever."

He climbed the porch steps and sat near her, the warmth of his body beside her a comfort that she, for some reason, needed right now. "That's good, right? You've been worried about him, and you must be so relieved to know he's doing okay."

"Yes, of course, but it sure doesn't make sense. He decides to live in an assisted-living facility and my mom has apparently decided to travel. On top of that, at some point, she started attending church again." She shook her head, turned toward him and explained, "None of that goes along with the two people I talk to on an almost daily basis. Something has happened, but I have no idea what."

Gavin twisted and pushed himself against the back of the porch, his long legs stretched in front of him as he regarded her, undoubtedly weighing what he was about to say. And Haley fought the impulse to scoot over and sit right next to him again. She liked the way it felt having him beside her, and she shouldn't. At least not as much as she did.

So she stayed put. And waited to see what her *friend* would say.

Buddy finished drinking and managed to get out of the water dish, then toddled across the porch, leaving wet paw prints in his wake. He climbed onto Gavin's lap and Gavin ran a hand along his back.

All the while Haley remained in limbo, knowing he would say something about the church comment, if nothing else. But Gavin didn't rush it. Instead he kept sitting there, looking at her and petting Buddy, as though debating whether to say anything at all. Finally she couldn't take it anymore, so she blurted, "What are you thinking?"

Instantly she gave herself a mental slap. The only times she'd ever asked guys that question was when she knew something was wrong, when the relationship was essentially over but the guy in question simply hadn't gotten around to telling Haley yet.

Gavin didn't say anything to dismiss her. Instead he said, "I'm thinking…it's pretty awesome that, in spite of the troubles she's faced, your mom has found her way back to God."

No accusations toward Haley on why *she* hadn't found her way back. No judgmental remarks or even questions on why her mother—and Haley—had decided it was easier to think God abandoned them than to admit they still needed Him.

"Are you always like that?" she asked softly. "Seeing the good in things instead of the bad?"

He continued rubbing Buddy's back. Bagel, seeing his sidekick getting attention, got up from his favorite sleeping spot on the porch and headed Gavin's way. "Now, you know better than that. Do I need to remind you about the day you met me? I was hardly seeing the good that day."

Which caused Haley to smile. He'd been a bigger grump than her grandfather. But then she remembered why. "It had been two years since you lost your family. You had every right to be…"

"A jerk?"

"A grouch. That was the word I was thinking."

Gavin laughed as Bagel climbed into his lap to squirm into place beside Buddy.

Haley was struck by how comfortable he looked here, sitting on her porch in the late afternoon with two puppies in his lap. She could get used to this.

He may have been rattled and angry that first day, but he looked so peaceful now. And she presumed that *this* was the norm for him. Peace, rather than dissatisfaction with the hand life had given him.

The hand *God* had given him.

"How did you do it?" she asked.

"How did I do what, exactly?"

"How did you keep from blaming Him, blaming God, when you lost them? When you lost your wife and your baby boy, why didn't you get angry at Him?"

"Who says I didn't?"

"You're at a children's home, a *Christian* children's

home, you're involved in the church and you have no problem at all talking about God at every opportunity," she said. "And I have it under good authority that you take notes during the service and that your comments are worthy of being heard."

He smirked at that. "Good authority?"

She lifted a shoulder. "Okay, Aaliyah."

The smirk shifted to an easy smile. "I do all of those things now, though I'm not certain about the comments being worthy to be heard, and I do find it easy to talk about God now, but I didn't then. In fact, I didn't for a year and a half."

He looked up at her and the orange glow from the setting sun cast a radiant gleam around him, as though God were telling her Gavin's comments *were* worthy to be heard.

"Being angry at Him, staying away from Him, didn't change what had happened, and it sure didn't help me deal with the pain. I turned away from the only One who could help, until a kid in my class at Memphis asked me to come to his church, because he had a part in a church play and wanted me to see his performance. I never missed attending a student's activity, but this was the first one who'd asked me to go to a church."

"So you went," Haley said.

"I did, and at the end of that service, they showed a video clip for Willow's Haven, for the need for foster parents, adoptive parents…and counselors."

The light around him seemed to grow brighter, or maybe that was because Haley was listening so intently. "You left teaching in Memphis to move here and be a counselor?"

"I knew that was what I was supposed to do. I didn't have my wife or my son anymore, but I still had a chance to have children. The children at Willow's Haven. I knew God put that on my heart, and that if I came here, I could help kids cope with losing…everything I had lost. Children who had lost their entire family, their entire world."

"Kids like Eli," she murmured.

He nodded. "Kids like Eli."

She was awestruck with how he'd turned his life around and found a way to make something good from a bad situation. And it made her own reasons for staying away from God…seem rather lame.

Yet she knew enough about God to know He could have stopped the heartache, could have eliminated at least some of the disappointments. If He wanted.

Then there was the fact she was certain that, if she was truly going to turn back to God, He would want her to forgive her dad. And forgiving Pierce Calhoun wasn't something she was prepared to do.

The sun dipped behind the mountains in the distance, the light that had illuminated Gavin fading, and a cold frisson trickled down Haley's spine.

As if Gavin sensed the change in her, that she couldn't say anything positive about her returning to God the way her mother had, he cleared his throat and started getting ready to leave. "You know, I'm sure the kids are back from the soccer game. I should head back so I'm there for the evening devo." He put the puppies down and stood, Buddy and Bagel moving toward her with his impending departure.

"Thanks for helping me today. And for letting me talk." Even if she knew he'd have liked for her to say more.

"Anytime." He started to leave, reached the porch steps and then paused. "Haley?"

"Yeah?"

"I didn't tell you what that sermon was about when I went to see that little boy in the church play."

"What was it about?" she asked, though she wasn't certain she wanted to know.

"How God never promised smooth sailing. He promised a safe landing."

## Chapter Twelve

"Miss Haley! Are you here? We've got some big news!"

Eli's yell echoed through the clinic.

Haley walked to the front and spotted Eli crouched on the floor behind the lobby counter petting his favorite puppy.

"I found Buddy," he said, and this time he didn't yell, since Buddy was snoozing. Little did he know, if his hollering didn't wake the pup, surely nothing else would.

"Yeah, he's been keeping me company up here, since Miss Aaliyah doesn't work today," Haley said.

"He's doing really good, isn't he?" Eli asked.

"Yes, sweetheart, he is." She crouched beside him as he continued petting the puppy, who indeed had experienced a complete recovery from the dehydrated, malnourished and neglected animal he'd brought in last week.

"Is he ready to go home now, then? 'Cause that's my big news." He was working hard to keep his voice down, but his sheer excitement caused even his whisper to project as moderately loud.

Buddy stretched, his tiny mouth opening wide in a yawn before he rolled over and went back to sleep.

"What's your big news?" Haley asked.

"I'll let Mr. Gavin tell you," he said, peering over Haley's head.

She hadn't needed Eli to tell her that Gavin was standing behind her. She'd sensed him, his bigger-than-life, abundantly masculine presence emanated from him, and somehow, Haley always knew when he was near.

And liked it. A lot.

"What's the big news?" she asked, taking in the way he leaned comfortably against the door, arms casually crossed, hair slightly mussed, his smile…sending a trail of goose bumps down her arms.

"Brodie and Savvy heard from Candace Yost today. She's the social worker for Willow's Haven. And she said she got approval for animals to visit the home over-night."

"Isn't that great, Miss Haley?" Eli asked. "Buddy can come spend the night with me tonight, and he'll get to be there for Ryan's party."

"Ryan's party? Is today Ryan's birthday?"

"No, ma'am," Eli said, his little mouth sliding to the side. "He's going to his new home and getting a new mommy and daddy." He drew his hazel eyes upward to lock with Gavin's. "But I'm not supposed to be sad, because it's a happy party, and maybe I'll still get to see him sometimes, 'cause he won't be very far away."

"That's right, buddy," Gavin assured him.

She could tell Eli was torn by the situation but was trying to be brave and strong and happy for his friend. Which made her feel even more compassionate toward this precious little boy. "I'm sure Buddy would love to go spend the night with you at Willow's Haven, and go to Ryan's party."

"That's great," he said, but his voice didn't seem quite as excited. Then he looked at Haley and said, "Ryan still loves his first mommy and daddy, but they're in Heaven, so God gave him a new mommy and daddy to have, too."

She blinked. Bit her lip. Worked hard to keep her throat from closing in completely. Those darling children at the home had been through so much—*Eli* had been through so much—and yet, despite everything, their faith remained strong and their hearts were still filled with hope.

"Miss Haley, can I have a purple balloon?" he asked, pointing toward the helium balloons she kept on hand for her youngest customers.

"A purple balloon?" she repeated, thankful that Eli hadn't continued his conversation about Ryan leaving, and mommies and daddies going to Heaven. "Sure, you can have any color that you want."

She moved to the sorting bin for the balloons and withdrew a floppy purple one.

"Here, I'll help." Gavin moved next to her and reached around her to get the scissors and curling ribbon. He brought his mouth to her left ear and whispered, "You okay?"

He had to stop doing things like that—getting so close to her, causing her to want to turn to him, to tell him how she felt each time he was near. Or ask if he could help. Or simply was…Gavin.

"I'm okay," she said softly.

"Can I get a piece of paper and a marker, Miss Haley? I need to write something." Eli had already moved to Aaliyah's skinny side cabinet, the one with the clear drawers on the front where coloring books, markers, crayons, stickers and paper were easily visible inside. Aaliyah had stocked the tiny cabinet for children who ended up having to wait in the lobby awhile.

"Yes, of course, Eli," she said, working the end of the balloon around the spout on the helium canister.

"Thank you." He pulled out a piece of paper as well as crayons, stickers and markers.

"He's such an amazing little boy, isn't he?" she whispered to Gavin as she watched Eli draw a heart on a page before she filled the balloon.

"Yes, he is," Gavin agreed. "And to have gone through so much and still know that God will take care of him, that's pretty incredible, don't you think?"

She knew what he was getting at, wondering why she hadn't turned to God during her tough times. "I almost went to the church yesterday," she said quietly.

He rested a jeans-clad hip on the counter beside her, leaned toward her. "I actually prayed for that."

She wasn't surprised. Over the past couple of weeks, she'd determined that quite a few people seemed to pray for her on a regular basis. She'd also determined that she didn't mind them praying on her behalf, after all.

"What kept you away?" he asked, his words delivered as softly as her own.

She glanced at Eli, saw that he had now grabbed a pencil and started writing what appeared to be a lengthy message, or perhaps a poem, at the bottom of the page. "I wanted to go, but I wasn't certain I should."

"Why is that?"

She nodded at the thin blue paperback book her assistant had given her. "I'm certain God put it on Aaliyah's heart to bring me that book. It's about Joseph and forgiveness."

He picked up the book, saw the page dog-eared near the middle. "Looks like you've been reading it."

"I have. It's tough, you know, to read the story of everything Joseph went through, and most of it due to his own brothers. And see how he forgave them."

"It's one of my favorites," he said. "In fact, I've used it a couple of times already in the daily devotions with the boys at Willow's Haven. Why is it tough for you to read?"

She knew he was smart enough to know why, but he must have sensed she needed to talk about it. And he was being a friend, caring and listening without judging.

"It's tough because I know I should be forgiving my father, and I just haven't been able to do it." She shook her head. "I don't know if I ever can."

"And that's what's keeping you away from the church? Away from God?"

She'd let the balloon slip off the spout while they were speaking and she turned away from Gavin to put it back on. Not because she felt hurried to get the balloon ready—Eli was clearly working hard on his project and wasn't paying them any attention anyway—but because she didn't want to look at Gavin. He'd see too much. Know too much.

She didn't want to voice the truth of her heart. That she felt she wasn't worthy of God's love.

His finger touched beneath her chin before she could start the helium and he lifted her face to look at his. "Hey," he said quietly, "there isn't anyone in that church who has it all right. That's why we're there, and that's why we pray…and trust in Him to love us, imperfections and all."

She forced a smile. "Maybe I'll come to the next service."

His finger still rested beneath her chin and he rubbed his knuckle gently back and forth as he leaned closer. "You don't have to be in the church building to get close to God, but I'm pretty sure you knew that already."

She did, of course, but she also hadn't known how to pray to Him again when she was still so very angry with her father. And at life in general. Or at least the fact that her life hadn't panned out the way she'd planned.

But then she scanned the scene before her. She was here, in her own clinic, with an amazing man at her side. No, he wasn't her husband, which would have been a big part of her dream, but he definitely cared about her, not only emotionally but also spiritually. And— she looked at Eli—she had a precious little boy who she absolutely adored. No, he wasn't her child, which would have been the other part of that dream, but she cared about him deeply.

And he cared about her.

She blinked. Her life wasn't the picture-perfect situation she'd planned for age thirty.

But it wasn't far from the mark.

"Miss Haley, I'm almost done. Is the purple balloon ready?"

She swallowed, grinning at Gavin. "Almost." Then she pressed down on the spout and filled the balloon. Deflated, the purple balloon looked almost black, but as the helium stretched it full, the black turned to a gorgeous deep purple. "How's that look?" she asked.

"Perfect!" he said as he started folding the paper accordion-style, so that it became a tiny bow tie–looking form, with only snippets of his coloring and stickers visible on the creases. "Can you put a red and blue ribbon on it, Mr. Gavin?"

"Red and blue?" Gavin asked. He had already selected a bright gold streamer and was about to cut it. "You don't want this gold one with the purple balloon?"

"No, it needs to be red and blue. Red and blue make purple, right?"

"That's right," Haley said, smiling as Gavin rewound the gold ribbon on the bolt and instead cut a long red and a long blue strand to tie on the end of the purple balloon.

Within seconds they had the balloon ready, completed to Eli's specifications.

"Okay, Eli, here you go," she said. "Do you want me to tie it to the chair here until y'all are ready to go?"

"No, ma'am. But can you tie this to it, like under the balloon part?" He held up the folded paper.

Gavin's eyebrows lifted and he seemed as confused as Haley by the request, but she answered, "Sure."

Eli got to his feet and brought her the folded page.

She took it, held it beneath the knot at the base of the balloon. "You want me to tie it here?"

"Yes, ma'am." He watched as she looped the curling ribbon around the letter then tied it in place, making the purple balloon look as though it were wearing a bow tie. "Okay, now do you want me to tie it up so it'll stay safe until you go?"

"No, ma'am. Can we take it outside now? Please?"

Gavin had sensed something going on in Eli's mind this afternoon. He'd suspected it had to do with his friend Ryan going to live with the family that planned to adopt him. Gavin had been waiting for Eli to say more about it, or about the party planned for Ryan, but he'd hardly said anything at all…until they'd got here and he'd shared the news with Haley.

Now he suspected that this balloon had something to do with Ryan. More than likely, Eli wanted to write a goodbye letter to his friend and, for some reason, wanted it tied to his balloon.

But taking it outside, especially on this windy afternoon, might not be wise if he wanted it to hold up until the party. However, the boy seemed determined.

"We can take it outside," Gavin said, "but we should probably tie it around your wrist first so it doesn't fly away."

Eli shook his head. "No, I need to hold it, please."

"O-kay," Gavin said, glad that Haley had plenty of balloons but not wanting Eli to lose the coveted letter. "Hold on to it tight."

Eli gave him a little smile. "Will you come with me, Mr. Gavin? And you, Miss Haley? And can you bring Buddy, so he can see?"

At some point while they were readying the balloon, Buddy had roused from sleep. Gavin leaned down to pick him up. "Sure."

They followed the child outside, where he walked around the corner of the building, the purple balloon trailing behind him. The breeze had grown even stronger, the balloon bouncing wildly as Eli struggled to hold on to the long red and blue ribbons.

"Eli, do you want me to hold the balloon for you?" Haley asked.

"No, ma'am."

He lifted his hand, the streamers dangling from his scarred fingers.

"Eli, be careful…" she warned.

He released the balloon.

Haley jumped forward in an effort to catch it, but the wind had it soaring quickly. She didn't make it far, anyway, because Gavin wrapped his arm around her and pulled her next to him.

"I think he's wanting to do this," he said against her ear, swallowing past the intimacy of whispering in her ear or holding her this close.

"Eli? Why did you let it go?" she asked.

Eli held his hand above his eyes, watching the purple balloon move higher and higher, appearing smaller and smaller as it climbed toward the clouds. "I needed to send my letter to Heaven."

Gavin glanced at Haley then at Eli. "Is that right, son?"

"Yup." He bobbed his head. "And Daddy's favorite color is blue, and Mommy's favorite is red. So they'll know the balloon is for them. And they can read my letter."

Gavin was glad he was holding Haley because he heard her quick intake of breath and felt her lean against him for support. Undoubtedly she was as impacted by Eli's tender gesture as Gavin. This sweet little boy had sent a letter to his parents…in Heaven.

"Eli," Gavin said slowly, struggling to harness the emotions evoked by his touching actions, "what did you write to them in your letter?"

"I told them about Buddy. And I drew them a picture of him."

Haley seemed to gather her composure. She cleared her throat. "That's—wonderful, Eli."

"And I told them about Ryan and how we're having his goodbye party. And how he's getting a new mommy and new daddy."

Haley sucked in another quick breath as Eli brought

his other hand up to help shield his eyes from the sun, setting over the mountain and causing the balloon to slowly but surely lose visibility.

"And I told them that, when I get a new mommy and a new daddy, I'll still love them, too."

# Chapter Thirteen

Haley unlocked the clinic at 5:30 a.m., well before she normally arrived. She'd given up on sleep two hours ago, tossing and turning with Eli's words about his parents echoing through her thoughts and dreams.

Each time she heard them, they were quickly followed by Gavin's.

*You don't have to be in the church building to get close to God.*

Her pillow had been damp with tears, her eyes opened to the truth.

God hadn't abandoned her.

She'd abandoned Him.

And she wanted Him back in her life, in her heart. More than that, she needed Him, to guide her and direct her through the biggest decision she'd ever made.

She loved Eli, with every bit of her heart, and she wanted to *be* the new mommy he'd told his parents about.

And she knew she needed God, yet she'd been too stubborn and hardheaded to admit it. All because she hadn't been willing to forgive.

*That's why we pray...and trust in Him to love us, imperfections and all.*

She wondered if Gavin had any idea how his words had penetrated her soul, reminding her of everything she'd missed over the past year. Not the perfect life that she'd dreamed of...but the perfect God that would never let her down.

She'd missed *Him.*

"You didn't move," she said to the One she knew listened to her heart. "I did."

Today she'd find out what she needed to do to start the process of adopting the little boy she had no doubt God had placed into her life for a reason. And she'd thank Gavin for opening her eyes and reminding her of what she needed most.

Last night she'd prayed, for the first time in over a year, and it hadn't been for her dreams to come true.

It had been for her God to have control of her life again.

"Help me, Lord," she whispered, turning on the lobby lights. "If it be Your will, let me be a mommy to Eli and give him what he needs. And thank You for Gavin. For the friend he is and for the patience he's had in leading me back to You."

Feeling positive, and a little overwhelmed, in the decisions she'd made through the night, she walked toward the front desk and prepared to start the day.

She withdrew her phone from her bag and noticed two texts that she hadn't seen last night. The first was from Savvy, in response to Haley's late-night text to her.

Brodie and I are so excited that you're interested in adopting Eli! Call us in the morning to discuss the steps involved.

She smiled, looking forward to telling Gavin of her decision to adopt the boy she'd grown to love. Then she read the second text, from her mom.

So sorry I haven't had a chance to call, but I'm fine. I have so much to tell you. I love you!

Clearly her mother had found joy again, found peace again. Found her way back to God again.

Haley tapped her response.

I love you! And we do need to talk—I have so much to tell you, too.

She was no longer overly concerned in the lack of daily phone conversations with her mom. True, she missed talking to her on a regular basis, but she was too pleased that her mother had found happiness and contentment to be disappointed that she hadn't called in a while. But she did look forward to telling her mom about Eli, the boy she loved. And about Gavin, the friend…she hadn't even realized she needed.

Haley wondered if—and how—her mother had forgiven her dad. No doubt, if she'd been able to do it, God had helped.

Turning to the desk, she spotted the thin bright blue paperback Aaliyah had given her positioned prominently in the middle of the counter.

She glanced at the clock. Three hours until the clinic officially opened.

Plenty of time to continue reading and, if she truly trusted in God to help, begin forgiving.

Gavin sat on the front porch of the cabin, his Bible in his lap as he watched the sun come up. He'd been awake for quite a while, reading his Bible and think-ing about everything that had transpired yesterday af-ternoon with Haley and Eli.

There was so much to process, to wrap his brain around, but the one thing he kept coming back to was that letter Eli had written to his parents. Undoubtedly, Haley had been affected as much as Gavin had been.

He closed his eyes, knowing how much he felt to-ward Eli but also wondering…

What did he feel toward Haley?

Because yesterday, as he'd held her and the two of them watched Eli send that message to Heaven, he'd felt…like they were one.

He shook his head. *God, help me. That isn't what I want. I can't go through that kind of relationship again, that kind of love again.*

*That kind of potential pain.*

How was he going to stop himself from getting closer and closer to this incredible woman? Especially when they both cared so much for Eli?

And…about each other?

He thought about her spraying him with paint, run-ning from him and him giving chase. He couldn't re-member the last time he'd had so much fun. He'd had nothing remotely similar since he lost Selah.

A stab of guilt pricked his heart. He'd been so de-termined to keep this relationship platonic. And it was, he supposed. But his thoughts kept hovering around all the moments he'd spent so far with the fascinating vet. And he didn't know how to make that stop. Because every day, the more time he spent getting to know her, the more he still wanted to know.

This was not good.

*God*, he prayed again, *help me.*

"Mr. Eli, something's wrong with Buddy!"

Gavin closed the Bible and put it on the table beside him, said a quick prayer that the puppy was okay and headed inside.

Every seven-year-old boy was gathered around Eli, who was crying as he held Buddy in his lap. "He—got sick, and he looks sad. Something's wrong!"

"What happened?" he asked as the circle of boys parted for him to get through.

"I heard him throwing up, and I went to take care of him, but he just keeps trying to throw up again."

Buddy's body shook and seemed to convulse, his stomach visibly tightening.

"Can Miss Haley make him better?" Eli asked tearfully.

Gavin certainly hoped so. "I'll take him to her right now." He grabbed a small afghan from the couch nearby and gently wrapped Buddy in it. "Let me tell Mr. Mark where I'm going."

"Can I go, too? Please, Mr. Gavin?" Eli cried. "Please? He'll be scared without me."

Gavin knew the one who was scared was the boy pleading with him now. He nodded. "Sure." Then he looked at the other boys. "You guys wait right here, and Mr. Mark will be here soon."

He headed out, Eli beside him. The morning chill was still in the air, typical for November, and Eli hissed in a shaky breath. Gavin had no idea whether it was because the child was cold or because he was terrified for his puppy, but he looked down and saw that Eli had left the cabin without shoes. Or a jacket. And he was still in his pajamas.

"Ryan!" Gavin called, and Eli's best friend hurried toward them.

"Yes, sir?"

"Get Eli his tennis shoes and his jacket for me, okay? Bring them to him in my truck." He walked to the truck and opened the door for Eli, then placed Buddy in his lap. "Take care of him for a sec while I tell Mr. Mark where we're headed, okay?"

Tears rolled down Eli's full cheeks. "Yes, sir."

Gavin jogged to the next cabin and quickly brought Mark up to speed. Then, while Mark called Brodie and they took over with the boys, he called Haley. He didn't want Eli hearing this conversation, but he wanted to give her a heads-up so she'd be prepared.

Haley hung up the phone and got ready for Buddy's arrival. From everything Gavin told her, and the fact that she knew Buddy had been fine when he left yesterday afternoon, she assumed the curious puppy had found something in the cabin and eaten it. Something he couldn't digest.

A common occurrence for nosey puppies. But also something that could be fatal, if she couldn't remove the obstruction. She couldn't bear the thought of Eli losing this puppy, and her mind quickly returned to the first day she'd met him.

*You can't let that puppy die.*

She'd been determined not to let that happen then, but she was even more determined now. Buddy meant the world to Eli. And Eli meant the world to Haley. And Gavin.

*Please, Lord. I need this puppy to be okay. In Your Son's name, amen.*

No sooner had she finished her prayer than she heard a car door slam outside. She hurried to the door and opened it in time to see Gavin helping Eli and Buddy exit the car.

"Miss Haley," Eli cried, "he needs help!"

"I know, sweetheart, I know." She scooped the puppy into her arms and saw his stomach convulsing. "I'm going to take a look at his tummy and try to figure out what's going on, okay?"

He nodded and Gavin wrapped an arm around him. "We'll hang tight in the lobby and see what Miss Haley can find out, okay?"

"We'll be praying," Eli said tearfully.

"That's good," she said. "And I'm praying, too."

At her words, Gavin looked up, those beautiful blue eyes filled with compassion and understanding. He had helped her find her way back to prayer again.

"I'll do my best with him," she said quietly.

He nodded. "I know you will."

Then he guided Eli to the lobby chairs while Haley took Buddy to the back so she could stabilize him and determine what was going on.

"Do you think he's going to be okay?" Eli asked, a question he'd repeated several times during the drive over and again as he and Gavin sat in the lobby.

"Dr. Haley is doing her very best to make sure he is. That's her job, and she's very good at her job."

Eli sniffed loudly and then leaned forward. "I hear her coming."

Gavin did, too, Haley's footsteps getting louder as she moved down the hall toward the lobby.

"What's that, Miss Haley?" Eli asked as soon as she appeared at the doorway.

She held an elongated X-ray in her right hand and brought it over to the two of them, crouching in front of Eli. "Eli, do you remember seeing any little round balls at the cabin, or maybe a marble?"

Eli looked at Gavin, his hazel eyes wide. "Ryan got marbles at his party last night. We were playing with them before bed."

Haley nodded slowly. "Okay, well, I think Buddy may have been a little too curious about one of those marbles. Let me show you." She held the X-ray up to the light. "This shows what's inside Buddy."

"I've seen X-rays in my science book. Is that the marble?" He pointed to the perfect circle that made it look like the X-ray had been hole punched in the center of Buddy's abdomen.

"I believe it is," she said. "And here's the tricky part. It looks like that marble is stuck there. And while it's there like that, Buddy can't eat or drink very well. I'm going to need to try to get it out."

"How do you get it out?" His voice wobbled, as if he knew what was coming. "Will he need surgery?"

"Yes, he will," she replied as Gavin wondered how the tiny puppy would fare through the operation. "But I've done this surgery before, because lots of puppies tend to eat something that looks like it might be food."

"So he'll be okay then?" Eli asked hopefully.

"I'm going to do my best."

Gavin appreciated that she didn't make any promises, but he also prayed that Buddy would be fine. "So should Eli go to school now?" he asked, knowing the answer but wanting Haley to tell the little guy so he wouldn't want to stay here all day. And worry about what was going on in the back.

"Yes, you should definitely go to school," she said. "Because the surgery will take some time and even after it's done, Buddy will need to rest. Tell you what, I'll call Mr. Gavin and let him know how Buddy is doing later today, and we'll see when it'd be good for you to come. Because I know he is going to want to see you as soon as he can."

"I want to see him, too," Eli said, a couple more tears slipping free and rolling down his cheeks.

"Come on, Eli." Gavin wrapped his arm around the boy and guided him out of the chair. "We'll go back to Willow's Haven and let you get dressed, then I'll check you in at the school."

"And you'll tell Mr. Gavin how Buddy is doing, so he can tell me right after school?"

"I promise I will." She started to stand, but Eli stopped her, leaning toward her and wrapping both arms around her neck.

"Miss Haley?"

"Yes, Eli," she answered gently. "What is it, honey?"

"I love you."

Gavin's pulse stuttered at the honest proclamation. He watched her expression change, her eyes grow misty and her mouth tremble, then she hugged Eli and kissed his tear-covered cheeks.

"Oh, Eli, I love you, too."

## Chapter Fourteen

By the time Gavin took Eli to change his clothes, fed him breakfast and took him to school, it was just past ten, and he still hadn't heard from Haley. How long did surgery on a puppy take? And how difficult was it to remove the marble?

As he climbed back into his car in the school parking lot, he couldn't stop blaming himself for what had happened. He'd seen the boys playing with the marbles and he'd helped Eli put Buddy's bed beside his last night when he went to sleep. But what had he been *thinking*? He should have known better than to leave a rambunctious pup where he could roam freely amid the toys and trinkets associated with seven-year-old boys.

*God, please let him be okay. And be with Haley as she cares for him.*

His phone rang and Brodie's name flashed across the display. "Hey, Brodie, what's up?"

"Eli make it to school?"

"Just dropped him off." Gavin knew that wouldn't have been why his boss had called. He'd just seen Brodie at Willow's Haven and he'd known Gavin and Eli were headed to the school.

"Good deal. I didn't want to say anything if he was still around you, didn't want to take a chance on him hearing it until it's all official, but I just wanted you to know how excited we are about Haley's decision. I'm sure you had something to do with it, and we think she'll be terrific."

Gavin had no idea what he was talking about. And another call kept beeping in while Brodie was speaking, so he thought he might have missed a key piece of information. "Terrific at what, exactly?"

"As a mom for Eli."

Gavin pictured that purple balloon with Eli's heartfelt letter, telling his parents how he would love them when he got his new mommy and daddy. Then he saw that same, adorable little boy hugging Haley and telling her...that he loved her.

"She will be terrific." He knew in his heart that it was true. What an amazing mother Haley would be.

*And an amazing wife*, his heart whispered.

He shook his head, dismissing the thought before it had a chance to settle.

"I agree," Brodie said. "So, have you heard anything about Buddy?"

"Not yet. I'll keep you posted if I do."

He disconnected then looked to see whose call he had missed. Haley Calhoun.

A text message from her came in while he was looking at the name on his display.

Tried to call but it went to voice mail. I wanted you to know the surgery went great. Marble is gone. Just waiting for Buddy to wake up now.

Leaning his head against the headrest, Gavin closed his eyes. "Thank You, God." Then he quickly tapped out a reply. Be right there.

He turned on the car and started the short drive to the clinic acutely aware of two things. One, while Haley had relayed the information about Buddy's surgery, she hadn't asked Gavin to come. And two, he was going anyway. In fact, he couldn't imagine anything that would keep him away.

Haley read Gavin's reply. Obviously he cared as much about Buddy as she and Eli did. She glanced at the puppy currently in the incubator to keep him from becoming chilled, saw his eyes squint as he started to wake.

She smiled. Eli was going to be so happy. She prayed she could always make him happy, especially when she told him that she wanted to be the new mommy he'd talked about.

*Mommy.*

She couldn't wait.

She'd called Brodie and Savvy as soon as the surgery ended. They'd wasted no time giving her the basics on the path to adoption. A course for fostering, since fostering Eli would be the first step. Then a social worker would meet with her, and with Eli, periodically as a court evaluated her for parenting.

But they hadn't seen any reason to think the process wouldn't go smoothly. And they'd suspected Eli might be *her son* by Christmas or Valentine's Day at the latest.

Two amazing days to celebrate her dream of having a child.

She bit her lip, recalling the other part of her dream. But then she shook that away. God was giving her a chance to raise a precious little boy as her own, and she was beyond grateful.

"Hey."

She jumped in her seat, turned toward the doorway, where Gavin leaned in, smiling. "I knocked and then called your name from the front. You must have something pretty intense on your mind."

"I do," she whispered, her skin growing warm at the mere sight of him. "Look." She eased her chair back so he could have a full view of the patient, still twitching his eyes as he slowly woke. "No more marble."

"How about that," he said quietly. "Must have been a pretty incredible doctor working on him to take care of him like that."

She smiled, the compliment settling in her chest and warming her completely. Amazing how Gavin Thomason affected her, even by merely speaking.

He'd be a great friend to have around when she was raising Eli. A father figure Eli could look up to. A guy that Haley would be around often all the while trying to remember that they were just friends.

She sighed. But could she really compartmentalize her feelings like that? Or was she just fooling herself?

Buddy's eyes flickered again and she stood, motioning for Gavin to follow her out of the room so they could keep him in his quiet environment.

They reached the lobby and moved to the counter, Gavin leaning one hip against the side and Haley hopping up to sit on top, so that they were at eye level.

"So our little marble eater is going to be okay?" he asked.

"He'll be a bit groggy for the next day or so, probably sleeping most of the time, and then he'll have to endure a bland diet for a few days."

"Nothing as flavorful as marbles?" he asked with a sly grin.

"Hardly." She laughed, wishing she hadn't noticed

the slight indention when he smiled, a tiny dimple in his left cheek she hadn't seen before. It added yet another degree of striking to the man.

"But he'll be good as new after he recovers, right?"

"He will, though we'll have to watch him pretty closely from now on."

"Why is that?" His smile dropped. Dimple disappeared. "Will this cause a problem for him in the future?"

"Not necessarily," she said, "but typically when a dog eats one obstruction, he's going to eat another."

And the dimple made a reappearance. "Ah, I get it. Repeat offenders?"

She laughed again, thoroughly enjoying how easy she found it to talk and laugh with Gavin Thomason. "Usually."

"Then I'd say you're right—we'll have to watch this mischievous critter real closely from now on, won't we?" he asked, placing a hand on her shoulder. "Or should I say that Eli's new *mommy* will have to keep an eye on him?"

Her pulse skittered. She'd planned to tell him, but she should've thought about the possibility that Brodie or Savvy would've mentioned it first. "You know? What do you think? Do you think I'll do okay?"

"I can't imagine anyone who'd be better."

"You believe that?" she asked, needing to hear it from someone. Moreover, needing to hear it from *Gavin*. Brodie and Savvy had both said the same thing, but for some reason his opinion carried more volume in her heart.

And she wouldn't overanalyze why.

"I do believe it," he said. "And I suspect that that

dream of yours, what you wanted by age thirty, is about to come true."

She tried to control her shock at his statement, but was certain all color had instantly drained from her face. "My dream?"

"You had planned on having children by the time you were thirty," he said gruffly, "hadn't you?" When she didn't answer, he continued, "I'm just guessing, but I'm assuming you are close to thirty…"

"I turned thirty last month," she whispered.

Gavin had thought he'd pegged her dream right because he had experience with that very goal. "That had been my original plan, too, a few years ago. I wanted to be settled, have a child, or two, by the time I was thirty," he confided.

"I'm guessing you're thirty?" she asked in the same tone he'd asked her the same question.

"I'll be thirty-two on Valentine's Day."

"I can see you as a Valentine's baby." She tilted her head and looked at him as though wondering what he'd looked like as an infant.

"I was an ugly baby," he confessed.

She laughed so hard she snorted. "Oh, I doubt that."

He smirked, not only at the comment but also at the cuteness of the sound she made when she laughed.

"Have you given up on your dream?" she asked, running her fingers along the end of her ponytail as she spoke.

Gavin wondered if her hair was as soft as it looked. He also wondered what it would look like uncontained.

She waited for his answer.

He shrugged. "I haven't necessarily given up on it. Sometimes dreams change a bit. But just because they may not look the way you originally intended, doesn't mean you can't still have them. I *have* my dream now."

"You…have it?" she asked, her hand drifting away from the ponytail, her confusion obvious.

He nodded, smiled. "I have *lots* of children at Willow's Haven. And I'll have the opportunity to touch many more kids over the years while I'm working there."

She chewed on her lower lip, seemed to think about what she was going to say. And then, finally, murmured, "I don't see why you couldn't touch lives at Willow's Haven…and still have your original dream. You would be an amazing dad, Gavin."

"And you," he said hoarsely, putting a finger beneath her chin, "are going to be an amazing mom." He smiled, almost not believing what he felt for the beautiful, intriguing lady. "I hope all your dreams come true, Haley."

She moved toward him, only slightly, and a thick wave of hair slid loose from her ponytail and fell in one long curl in front of her right eye and cheek. She didn't seem bothered by the obstruction, but Gavin touched the soft, springy ringlet and gently tucked it behind her ear.

"Gavin," she whispered, her luminous eyes connecting with his.

He didn't stop to think as he followed an instinct he hadn't experienced…in over two years. Instead he closed the distance between them, his mouth finding hers and slowly sampling the sweetness of apples and cinnamon…and Haley Calhoun.

## Chapter Fifteen

"I had a good thing, and I blew it," Gavin said, ready to kick himself for letting the moment, the impulse, get away from him yesterday afternoon. He placed another piece of wood on the chopping block and split it in two.

Mark added the cut pieces to their growing pile then grabbed the next log for the block. "You keep saying that, but you still haven't told me *what* you did."

Gavin hadn't stopped expressing his frustrations with himself, but he hadn't wanted to tell the masses how badly he'd messed up with Haley.

Yet he was ready to talk. And somehow, try to repair the damage. Maybe Mark could provide advice on how to make that happen.

"Bottom line, I kissed her," he muttered, letting the splitting ax fall and two more pieces hit the ground.

This time, the other man made no move to pick them up. "You kissed who? Haley Calhoun, I'm guessing?"

It'd be better if he could somehow control his grin.

"This *isn't* a good thing." Gavin picked up the pieces himself and slung them on the pile.

"Oh, I'd be very surprised if it wasn't."

Gavin wasn't going to touch that by divulging details.

Truthfully, the kiss…had rocked him to the core. He'd replayed it continually since it had happened.

He'd probably be replaying it the rest of his life.

It was *that* perfect.

So perfect, in fact, that he hadn't wanted it to end.

And he couldn't stop thinking about what it'd feel like to do it again. Hold her again. Cradle her face in his hands, look into those amazing green eyes and—

He. Needed. Help.

Gavin picked up another hunk of wood, since Mark had perched himself on the stacked pile and just sat there grinning from ear to ear, his arms folded across his chest, instead of helping Gavin chop wood. Or work his way out of this mess. "You don't have any recommendation for how to fix this? Preferably before I have to take Eli to the clinic this afternoon to see Buddy?" He lifted the splitting ax, let it fall, then stepped back as one of the cut pieces nearly hit his foot.

"What is there to fix? I'd say you're finally on the right path."

"I'm not. I didn't want this to go beyond friends. Don't want any relationship to." He wasn't all that used to opening up, but his fellow counselor clearly didn't get it, so he explained. "Yesterday, I told Haley about my plans for age thirty, how I wanted to be settled down and have kids by then."

"O-kay," Mark said, still not seeing the problem.

"The thing is, those weren't merely my plans. They'd been my dream…with Selah. And I can't do that to her. Think about those types of things, have those kinds of feelings, with someone else." He shook his head. "I can't."

"But you are, aren't you? There isn't anything wrong with—"

"No. I've heard it all before and I don't want to hear it again." Gavin handed the splitting ax to his friend. "I don't want another relationship. I don't want to start over and risk everything again. And Haley deserves someone that can go all-in. That isn't me. We could be great friends, and I need to see if we still can, if I didn't ruin that completely yesterday." He nodded at the rest of the wood. "Can you handle this without me?"

Mark smirked. "Like I need your help to chop wood. Is a bluebird blue? Where are you going?"

"To try to get things back to the way they were before that kiss."

Mark whistled. "Yeah, I wouldn't hold my breath."

Haley's heartbeat kicked it up a notch, or ten, when Gavin entered the clinic as she handed Landon Cutter a bag containing Roscoe's monthly meds.

"Hey!" she said and then wished she hadn't practically screamed her excitement at seeing him. She hadn't stopped thinking about how very much she'd wanted that kiss and about how very much it'd rocked her to her core. It had felt so…right. Like a dream—her dream—coming true.

She'd been watching the door all day, anxiously waiting to see him again.

He smiled, a little awkwardly, which she thought was adorable. They'd have to wade these new waters carefully, learn how to balance their friendship along with their new relationship, the one that included long, amazing, knee-weakening kisses.

Haley's hand drifted to her mouth and she fought the urge to giggle. Life had certainly taken a blissful turn yesterday, and she couldn't wait to see what awaited them down this brand-new road.

"Gavin, good to see you," Landon said. "I was just leaving."

"Good to see you," Gavin replied. "I—came to check on Eli's dog, Buddy."

Odd, Haley thought, that he felt the need to provide an explanation for coming to see her. But also sweet. As though he was shy about the fact that they would undoubtedly be seeing even more of each other, as they had moved beyond the "just friends" boundaries they'd previously set.

All in God's time. Wasn't that what everyone had said to her, about why she'd never found the right man? She should've trusted God the whole time, because, clearly, He had something better in store.

Gavin.

Landon turned to Haley. "Thanks again, Doc Calhoun."

"You're welcome." She watched him leave, the door closing behind him, and then the realization that she was, once again, alone with Gavin hit her.

"I— How is Buddy?" His nervousness melted her heart. Had he also replayed that kiss over and over again throughout the night…and had he also seen a new vision for his future? One that included more than friendship and maybe all their dreams fulfilled?

"Buddy is doing great," she said. "You want to come see him?"

He visibly swallowed, shifted from one foot to the other. "Sure."

She led the way to the back and couldn't help but notice how he looked even more masculine today, wearing a flannel shirt, sleeves rolled up to the elbows, well-worn jeans and hiking boots. She loved the sheer maleness that accompanied everything about Gavin

Thomason. She'd known he would prove to be an amazing father figure for Eli.

But he'd also make an amazing dad.

She tried to control how quickly her heart was putting the cart before the horse. Slow. They'd need to take this slow. Because he hadn't even wanted a relationship again, until yesterday.

But she could be patient. Her happily-ever-after was certainly worth the wait.

"There's our little man," she said, grinning at Buddy. "He's still a bit groggy, but doing much better today."

"The IV is gone," he noted.

"Yeah, he's really doing well. I'm sure he'll be even better this afternoon when Eli visits."

Gavin moved to the puppy, tenderly touched his finger to his forehead and Buddy nuzzled against it. "You're a good boy, aren't you?"

"He is," Haley agreed. "Just need to keep him away from the marbles, or probably anything else that he might ingest." She smirked. "Which may prove to be a challenge."

"We can handle it," he said, and she liked the way he'd said *we*. Then she looked at him, and he wasn't smiling. In fact, he was frowning.

"Something happen with Eli?" she asked, concerned.

"No, nothing with Eli," he answered, but she could tell he had something on his mind.

"Come on, we'll go back up front and you can tell me."

They walked to the lobby and he moved to the same spot where he'd been yesterday, leaning against the counter. Haley, likewise, hopped up on top of the counter next to him, exactly where she'd been when they'd kissed.

"Aaliyah is working today, but she shouldn't get here for about a half hour." She wanted to let him know they had a little time to talk privately. And for him to kiss her again, if he was so inclined. Her heart fluttered in anticipation. "What is it?"

"Haley..." he said slowly.

Her nerve endings instantly bristled against her skin. She knew that tone. Had heard it before.

Too many times.

She blinked, not wanting to even ask him to finish whatever he was about to say. She knew before he confirmed it with his words.

He'd...changed his mind.

"I..." he started.

She held her breath.

"I...don't know what I was thinking yesterday afternoon. Or rather, what I was doing. I shouldn't have kissed you." He looked away from her, shifted his position against the counter so that he wasn't even inferring closeness to her, already putting distance between them. "I meant it when I said I can't offer more than friendship, and I know... I know that was your plan, too."

"My plan changed," she blurted then wished she could stuff the words back in.

He looked at her, those clear blue eyes filled with... regret. "Haley, I'm sorry. I—don't want that again. And I can't... I can't give you any more than friendship."

She fought the way her eyes instantly burned at the edges. She *wouldn't* cry. She couldn't let him see how badly he'd hurt her now. She cared too much for him to let him feel like he was shattering her heart.

Even if he was.

"Listen, we're going to have to see each other, with Eli and the animal program at Willow's Haven, and with living in such a small town…" A muscle ticked in his jaw. "And I think too much of you, Haley, to want our friendship, what we've shared together, to just end. But I need to know…can we still have that? After yesterday? Is there any way that we can still be friends?"

*No*, her heart whispered. *Definitely, absolutely, not.*

But if she said no then that meant no relationship at all with Gavin.

And she loved him. She knew it with every fiber in her being. Somewhere along the way, regardless of how she'd fought him, she'd gotten too close. Learned too much about the man. Wanted him to be more than a friend. More than an acquaintance. She wanted him in her life. And in her brand-new life with Eli as her son. She wanted him to be *their* son.

But she couldn't bear the thought of not being with Gavin in some way.

Even if that meant merely as friends.

"Yes," she whispered, hoping he would leave quickly, before the tears came. "We can be friends."

He sighed thickly, moved toward her and wrapped his arm around her in a hug.

She inhaled, drank in the clean, masculine scent of him, the feel of him holding her close.

Then he stepped away and a chill she'd never felt before flooded through her.

"Okay. I'll see you this afternoon, right? When I bring Eli?"

She nodded. "Sure. I'll see you then."

And she watched him leave, her happily-ever-after evaporating with every step. And those tears she'd been holding back trickling free.

## Chapter Sixteen

"Do you think Buddy will still get to come stay with me sometimes, if I make sure to put all of the marbles and things like that away?" Eli asked as Gavin drove him to the clinic after school.

"I'm sure he will." Gavin looked forward to the moment when Eli learned that Buddy would most likely live with him full-time soon. He would have a whole host of other animals, too—all the occupants of Haley's farm—when she adopted him.

She was going to make a great mother.

He swallowed. She'd also make a great wife. And some guy would undoubtedly find that out one day. Women like Haley didn't come along every day, and a guy would be a fool not to realize that.

Gavin took a deep breath, let it out. Mark had said those very words to him less than an hour ago when Gavin had told him about resetting the boundaries of their relationship and moving them back to being just friends.

One of the hardest things he'd ever done.

But the right thing. He didn't want a relationship and she hadn't wanted one, either.

*My plans changed.*

Those three words had hit him like a bucket of ice water. While Gavin had seen yesterday's kiss as a big mistake, she'd seen it as a new direction for their relationship. He'd noticed the sheen of tears she tried to hide, and it gutted him. But thankfully she'd also decided that they could remain just friends, not only for themselves but also for Eli.

"Aw, Miss Haley's truck is gone. Do you think she had to go take care of another animal? Do you think Buddy is still here?"

Aaliyah's vehicle was in one of the employee spots, but as Eli had noted, Haley's spot was vacant. "She may have had to go to a farm to take care of someone else's animal, but Miss Aaliyah's here, and I'm sure Buddy is, too. We'll see Miss Haley later, okay?" He hoped they did, anyway. He was a little apprehensive about it, truth be told, because things might be awkward as they worked past the boundary he'd crossed yesterday.

But it could be done.

He parked the car and Eli climbed out and darted inside.

"Hey, Miss Aaliyah! Can I see Buddy?"

Gavin heard her answer while he was still walking in.

"Of course, Eli. I'll take you to where he is. Miss Haley had to leave for a little while, but she wanted me to let you know she's coming to see you later at Willow's Haven, and that she's going to take you out for a special treat tonight."

Gavin entered in time to see Aaliyah leading him to the back. She glanced at him, cast an angry glare his way.

Not good.

A moment later she returned. "Buddy is doing better, well enough for Eli to hold, so he's bonding with him now. Haley left. She didn't want to be here when you got here," she said, her voice sharp and her words clipped. "She asked me to give you this." She walked to her desk, grabbed an envelope and snapped it toward him.

"Okay." He took the envelope, moved to one of the lobby chairs and withdrew the single sheet of paper.

Dear Gavin,

I know I said we could still be friends, but I was wrong. I can't. I told you the truth. My plans changed. And seeing you any more than absolutely necessary will only remind me of yet another shattered dream. I know God has a plan for me, and I get that it doesn't include you. But that doesn't mean I need reminding of that on a daily basis.

I'm telling Eli about wanting to adopt him tonight and letting him know he can start staying with me some while I go through the process. I want him to know that he is loved and that I want—desperately—to be his new mommy. And I can be happy with this new dream, with me and the little boy God is blessing me with. But that happiness will be hindered if I keep seeing the big dream every day. And you, whether you realize it or are willing to admit it, were the one I dreamed of.

I think the world of you. I always will. But I can't be "just friends."
Haley

Gavin stared, thunderstruck by how much a single kiss had cost him. He'd ruined a good thing. A great thing. The chance to have an amazing friendship with an even more amazing woman.

Not to mention a meaningful relationship with her and her future son, a boy he'd come to love.

Now she only wanted to see him when absolutely necessary?

"You messed up." Aaliyah stood on the other side of the counter, arms crossed, eyes glaring. "You royally messed up. And you hurt her. That's *not* okay."

No, Gavin knew that it wasn't, but he also knew he couldn't fix it. He couldn't give Haley what she wanted, because that was more than he was prepared to give. Now, or ever. So he didn't respond. Just folded the letter, slid it back into the envelope…and realized that, once again, his life was definitely *not* okay.

Haley arrived at Willow's Haven as nervous about seeing Gavin as she was about telling Eli about her desire to adopt him and be his new mommy.

"God, stay with me," she whispered, parking the truck and getting out.

She'd hardly taken two steps, though, when Eli dashed toward her. "Hey, Miss Haley! Did you bring Buddy?"

"Not this time, sweetie. He's still resting after his surgery, but it won't be long until I can bring him along again. Tonight, though, it's just me."

"Okay," he said, but didn't sound disappointed, and she was thankful for that. "Miss Aaliyah said you were taking me for a special treat! Is it ice cream?"

She laughed. "Well, it can be. I had actually thought we would go to the Sweet Stop on the square, and I'm pretty sure they have ice cream."

"They do! Is Mr. Gavin coming with us? He went

to talk to Mr. Brodie and Miss Savvy, but I can go ask him if he wants to come."

"Nah, that's okay. This is a special treat just for you," she said, not quite ready to see Gavin again yet. And, truthfully, not sure she'd ever be ready.

"Okay," he replied. "I'm excited. Are you excited?"

"I'm *so* excited." She smiled as she climbed into the truck with the little boy, who would soon be hers. She glanced toward Brodie and Savvy's cabin, thought about the man inside. The one who wanted to be her *friend*.

"Miss Haley, are you ready to leave?" He snapped his seat belt into place.

"Yes," she said, "I'm ready to go."

Gavin lifted the edge of the curtain at Brodie's front window, watching Eli and Haley pull away.

"Are you sure about this?" Brodie asked.

He dropped the curtain and turned back to the couple who had been so welcoming to him and had showed him the joy of taking care of children. He still wanted that but, like he'd told Haley, his dreams had changed. He could have kids of his own, lots of them, in fact, at a children's home.

Just not this one.

She'd decided they couldn't be friends. She'd also decided to keep her distance from him when possible, which would be practically impossible in a town the size of Claremont.

He didn't want to put her through that. Didn't want to hurt her every time he ran into her around town. And, if he stayed, he'd want to have a part in Eli's life, and that would only hurt Haley, too.

So he'd emailed the home in Oregon to see if they

still needed counselors. They did, and he'd made the decision. "I'm sure."

"I know you've only been here a short time," Brodie said, "but you've really made a difference in these kids' lives. Especially Eli's."

Gavin's heart constricted at the thought of leaving the little boy he adored. "He's going to be fine. He's getting a great new mommy."

Savvy had been listening in silence but she leaned forward in her chair and said, "I'd kind of thought he might be getting a new daddy eventually, too."

Gavin's jaw clenched. He couldn't be that daddy. Or the husband that Haley wanted. His heart just couldn't withstand that kind of relationship again.

"They said I can start immediately, if that's okay with y'all. I don't want to leave you in a bind, but me staying…it won't be good for Eli."

*Or for Haley.*

Brodie frowned. "Hey, man, if you need to go, we will make things work here. We've been short staffed before, and I can take over with your cabin until we find someone. But if you ever change your mind, you've got a job here, right, Savvy?"

"You should just stay," she said quietly. But when Brodie looked her way, she amended, "You will *always* have a job here, Gavin. The kids love you."

"I appreciate that." He loved the kids here, too. Loved the job. However, he couldn't hurt Haley by sticking around. "I'll plan to leave tomorrow, after the kids head to school."

"You will tell them goodbye, though, right?" Savvy asked. "A lot of them never get that kind of closure from their families, and you've already become like family to many of them, especially Eli, so you really need to tell him goodbye."

Gavin's stomach pitched but he nodded. He didn't want to tell Eli goodbye, but he would. She was right. He needed that. "I will."

He left their cabin and, the next morning, left a little of his heart behind.

# Chapter Seventeen

"Miss Haley! Someone's coming!" Eli ran around the barn, where Haley had been repairing the wiring on the rabbit hutch, this time wearing gloves.

She recalled the last time someone had been coming when she was working on the hutch. And the way Gavin had taken care of her wound. It had been the first time he'd put his arm around her.

He'd been gone for two weeks. And she didn't expect him to return.

Still…with Eli's announcement, her heart fluttered.

What a great Thanksgiving surprise that'd make, if he'd come back, for good.

"It's not Mr. Gavin," Eli said glumly. He'd been hoping Gavin would return ever since he'd left. "It's a man and a woman."

Fighting back her own disappointment, Haley removed the gloves, placed the pliers on a barrel nearby and walked to the front of the barn. She wasn't expecting any visitors and couldn't imagine who it could be.

"Well, hello there, little man." The lady's voice resonated…and went straight to Haley's heart.

"Mom?" She picked up her pace, hurried to see the

woman walking toward the barn. Her hair was piled on top of her head in her trademark do, blond ringlets in front of each ear. Long earrings and a matching necklace completed a stylish ensemble of a flowing sheer floral cardigan over autumn-toned slacks and short boots.

Her mother had a style of her own and Haley adored every bit of it.

"I had no idea you were coming!" she exclaimed, jogging toward her mom and wrapping her in a hug. "I thought you said you'd be in Charleston for Thanksgiving."

"Oh, we were, dear, but then we decided we'd rather spend the holiday with people we love."

Haley had been updating her mother on the adoption process and had told her how Eli would be spending his Thanksgiving break with Haley. "I'm so glad you came."

Eli had followed Buddy, who always took off running whenever a car approached. He'd caught the puppy near the house and was now walking back toward them.

"Eli, this is my mom."

He gave her a big grin. "Hey, I'm Eli."

Haley's mom moved a hand to her chest. "Oh, my, you're just as cute as Haley said."

"Thanks!" He smiled even bigger. "She's going to be my new mommy. Did you know that?"

"I did," she said, her eyes watering with her words. "And how do you feel about that?"

"I love Miss Haley," he said matter-of-factly, "so, I'm happy!"

"Of course you are," her mother said. Then to Haley she said, "He's absolutely adorable."

"Thanks." Pride ebbed through Haley at the special

little boy. Then she recalled Eli's original announcement. And the fact that her mother had said "we" were in Charleston. "Mom, who's with you?"

Her mother cleared her throat and turned toward the front of the house, where a tall, handsome man, who looked much younger than sixty-two, stood. He had his hands in his pockets and a slight smile on his face. "Hey, Haley Bug."

*"Dad?"*

"We didn't want to tell you everything over the phone," her mother quickly explained. "I wanted to make sure you understood when we filled you in on… well, everything."

"You're Miss Haley's dad?" Eli asked, always paying attention.

"I am," her father said.

"Are y'all going to be here for Thanksgiving tomorrow? 'Cause I need to make some more Pilgrim hats if you are."

"We would like to," her mother said. "In fact, we thought we might stay here for a little while, maybe until Christmas, if that's okay. We're retired now, you know."

Haley honestly felt like the earth had shifted beneath her feet, feeling as woozy as she had that day when she'd cut her hand and needed Gavin's help.

She could sure use his help now in dealing with… whatever this was.

"Eli, why don't you go make some more hats, just in case?" she asked.

"Yes, ma'am," he said and darted inside.

"Mom, what's going on?" she asked.

Her mother wrapped her arm around her and guided her toward the porch, alongside the man whom Haley, until a few short weeks ago, had never wanted to see again.

But this was her father. And she had forgiven him in her heart. Obviously her mother had, too.

But there was a huge piece of that story Haley didn't understand.

"Daddy?" Haley questioned.

He cleared his throat but then her mother shook her head. "No, Pierce. This is on me, for the most part, so I should explain."

"I don't get it. How is this on you?" Haley looked from her mother to her father and back again.

Her mom sighed deeply. "I didn't exactly tell you all of the truth over the past year," she admitted. "I was just so angry at your dad that I couldn't."

They'd taken a seat on the old wooden pew on one side of her porch. Her father moved to the rocker near Haley's mom and took her hand in his. "You had every reason to be."

Her mother squeezed his hand, blinked past her tears. "Oh, I know I did, at first. But then—" she looked at Haley "—he came to me, a month after everything happened, and told me he'd made a mistake. Pleaded with me to forgive him. And I—" she lifted a shoulder "—I told him I didn't want to ever see him again."

"And I knew she meant it, but…" He looked adoringly at his wife. "I couldn't give up on us. I had ruined it. I knew that. But I still loved her. I made a horrible mistake, and all I could do was keep begging her to forgive me. And keep coming back."

Her mom's mouth eased into a smile. "He was rather relentless. Wouldn't leave me alone. Even convinced your grandfather that he would be happy in an assisted-living home and that we might have a chance to revive

our marriage if he would quit monopolizing my time."
She laughed at that. "I'm really surprised he went along
with it, but he actually ended up liking the place."

"I could tell," Haley said. In fact, she'd been talking
with him regularly, thanks to Ivalene commandeering
his phone on a daily basis and dialing Haley's number.

"It took a year, but I finally convinced her to take a
chance on me—take a chance on *us*—again."

"It was tough to say no," her mother admitted, "especially when all of his church friends started singing
his praises."

"*His* church friends?" Haley asked, blown away by
so many revelations at once.

"That was what I had to get right first," her father
said. "I needed to get back to God, let Him lead me in
the right direction. And then—only then—could I find
myself worthy of your mom again."

"He got involved in a church back home, and then
he started talking to them, confessing what he'd done,
all the pain he inflicted, and how he wanted me to take
him back. He asked them to call me and plead his case."
She shook her head, but smiled. "They were quite relentless, too."

"And ever since she's given me another chance, I've
been trying to make sure she takes all of those trips and
sees all of those things she's always wanted to see." He
smiled, touched his finger to her chin, the way Gavin
had touched his finger to Haley's. "This past weekend,
we went back to Charleston, where we were married,
and renewed our vows."

"Isn't that something?" her mother asked.

"Yes," Haley said softly, "it is."

"Your mom has forgiven me, Haley, but I wanted to
ask if you would, as well. I have no excuses, but I can

promise you that I will do my best to never hurt your mother, or you, again. Will you—forgive me?"

She brushed her tears away and said honestly, "I already have."

Eli rushed onto the porch with Buddy in his arms and Bagel at his feet. "I made y'all some Pilgrim hats. You're going to have Thanksgiving with us, right?"

"Can't imagine anything we'd rather do," they said.

Haley sniffed, thinking life couldn't get much better.

Then she realized it could, but the man of her dreams was on the other side of the country, with no plans on coming back.

Gavin ate another bite of turkey, but he didn't taste a thing. The group home was beautiful, much larger than Willow's Haven, with multistory cabins that each housed at least twenty children and several counselors.

The kids were great, though he hadn't learned yet which cabin he'd be assigned to permanently. There was a two-month training period where his abilities would be assessed and he'd be matched with the best cabin for his talents.

The home was well organized and run meticulously. And he'd have the opportunity to be involved with many more children here.

But it wasn't Willow's Haven.

And none of the little boys was Eli.

And he missed Haley. Terribly.

Jared, one of his fellow counselors, pointed a crescent roll toward him from across the table. "Hey, man, it's Thanksgiving, and you look like you lost your best friend."

A very accurate assessment. His best friend…and

more. Had he done the right thing, leaving Claremont? Leaving Eli?

Leaving *Haley*?

Gavin forced a smile. "You're right. It's Thanksgiving. And I have a lot to be thankful for."

"When you're done, you should head outside and see what the kids are doing. That'll cheer you up."

Gavin didn't want another bite. "Think I'll head on out now." He saw the counselors and kids gathered in small groups near every exit, but he hadn't known what holiday activity they were participating in. When he got to the door, however, he saw the baskets of markers and small sheets of paper.

"Here you go," one of the teen boys said, handing him a white slip of paper. "You write some things you're thankful for, and then take it outside."

Gavin took the tiny slip and moved to a small table, away from the crowd. It didn't take him but a moment to write what he was most thankful for.

*God. Christ.*

He paused, his jaw flexing at the truth of the next two on his list. He could keep from writing them down, but he'd be lying. So he continued.

*Haley and Eli.*

Who was he kidding? He didn't want the pain of loving again, the way he'd loved Selah and their son, because he didn't want to betray their memory. And he didn't want to risk losing that kind of love again.

But Selah and their baby would always be in his memories and he would always love them. The way Eli would always love his first mommy and daddy, like he'd put in that heartfelt letter he'd sent to Heaven.

Gavin…loved that little boy. Wanted to be his new daddy. He knew that with absolute certainty.

And he loved Haley. Not as a friends-only kind of way, but in a till-death-do-us-part kind of way.

He folded the piece of paper and went outside with the other paper-yielding folks.

And that's where he saw the balloons. Hundreds of balloons of all colors. One of the teen girls came up to him and handed him one. "You tie what you're thankful for to the balloon and let it go," she explained. "Our phone number and email for the home is on the back of the page, and we'll see how far your note travels. It'll let the person who finds it know what you're thankful for, and remind them to be thankful, too."

He glanced up at the big, fat purple balloon she'd handed him. Then he tied his note to the ribbon and let it fly.

He had no idea how far a balloon would travel from Oregon and doubted that it would make the trip to Alabama.

But his message, what he was most thankful for, needed to be delivered. And Gavin knew what he had to do to make that happen.

## Chapter Eighteen

"Mr. Gavin! You came back!" Eli ran full blast from the barn toward Gavin's car on Saturday afternoon.

Gavin was spent. He'd left Thursday and had only stopped to sleep briefly during the thirty-seven-hour drive. But just seeing that little boy, hearing the loudest voice he'd ever imagined for a seven-year-old, sent a surge of adrenaline through his body…and pure joy to his soul.

He climbed out of the truck in time to catch Eli, hurling himself into his arms, with Buddy, running and barking behind him and Bagel howling from the front porch. Sterling even issued a noticeable neigh from the barn at his arrival.

The only one he didn't see was the one he needed to see most of all.

Gavin released a ragged breath. He needed to apologize. To confess his faults.

And his love.

"Hey, there," he said, hugging Eli and kissing the boy's cheek. "I've missed you."

"I've missed you," Eli said, laughing. "And I think Miss Haley missed you, too."

"You do?" he asked thickly. "Did she say that?"

"No, but I think she did."

His hopes slipped a little. "Okay, then. Is she in the house?"

"She's not here right now," a man said, stepping off the porch. He was older, with charcoal hair and a bit of silver at the temples. Distinguished looking, even if he was currently wearing a long-sleeved T-shirt and jeans. There was a tool belt strapped around his waist and he had a hammer in one hand. "You're Gavin, I'm guessing?"

"Yes, sir, he's Mr. Gavin," Eli answered. Then he looked to Gavin and said, "That's Mr. Pierce. He's Miss Haley's daddy."

A woman walked out onto the porch rubbing her hands on a dish towel. "Pierce, is someone here?"

Gavin didn't have to ask. Haley was the spitting image of her mother. "Mrs. Calhoun?"

"Yes, that's Miss Haley's momma," Eli informed him. "This is Mr. Gavin!" Eli yelled to the lady.

"Ah, I see," she said, exchanging a knowing look with her husband.

Gavin must not have controlled his surprise quickly enough, because the man's mouth slid into a grin. "Yeah, I guess she told you about me, but you should probably also know that Haley's mom—and Haley—have forgiven me."

"After I made him eat a bit of humble pie," the woman said, which caused her husband to wrap an arm around her and grin.

"Well-deserved humble pie."

Gavin looked toward the driveway, wondering when Haley would also make an appearance.

"She's not due back for a while," her father said.

"She went to the Cutter farm to check on the animals there. Their dog had gotten into a tussle with a skunk, I think. And then she said she needed to go check on the animals at the clinic. She has a few boarded there for the holiday."

"Right," Gavin said, disappointed she wasn't here.

"I'm sure she hasn't made it to the clinic yet," her mother said, "if you wanted to go and meet her there. And talk."

Gavin grinned, looking to her folks. "Thanks." He hugged Eli again. "I'll be back to see you in a little bit, okay?"

"Are you staying forever?" His hazel eyes were wide and filled with…hope.

"That's what I want, Eli," Gavin said honestly, "more than anything. It just took a little time for me to figure that out."

Haley had thought she would have a leisurely day at home. Helping her dad as he made repairs on her porch railing. Watching her mom utilize her culinary skills in transforming the Thanksgiving leftovers into some mystery masterpiece. Enjoying the last of her Thanksgiving break with Eli.

Then Roscoe had proved, once again, to be her best customer when he'd managed to get into a fuss with an angry skunk. It'd taken Haley, Landon, Georgiana and Abi a good hour of scrubbing to de-skunk the Lab. Thankfully, Haley'd already had the solution mixed and ready at the clinic and they'd had Roscoe back to normal in a jiff.

After texting her folks to let them know her plans, she stopped by the clinic to check on her boarded pets before coming home. It felt good seeing her parents together, introducing them to Eli and being a real family again.

Haley had so thought she would have that kind of family for herself, but she was very blessed with Eli. The two of them would do just fine, even if they both had a huge hole in their hearts left by the handsome counselor.

She lifted the flower pot, got the key, unlocked the front door and stepped inside.

"You really should find a better place to hide your key."

The key fell to the floor. "You're...here?"

"I am." Gavin leaned against the counter, looking as ruggedly handsome as ever, in the very spot that he'd been a few weeks ago when he'd held her close and...

She couldn't let her mind go there. Couldn't let herself hope. Not until she knew for sure why he'd returned.

"I always wanted to see you with your hair down," he said. "You're so very beautiful, Haley."

"Why...?" she whispered. "Why...are you here?"

His smile lifted, but he seemed hesitant, so she held her ground. She couldn't bear the thought of assuming anything and having him tear her apart again.

He eased away from the counter and started toward her. "I realized you were right," he said softly.

She moistened her lips, said a quick prayer for God to stay with her...and that she wasn't dreaming. "I was right? About what?"

"About it being dangerous." He crossed the floor, slowly but surely closing the distance between them. "You said getting close to you was dangerous, because I might decide I can't live without you," he murmured, stroking his fingers against her cheek then gently tunneling them through her hair.

Haley did her best not to faint. This wasn't a dream. But it was *her dream*.

"And I can't, you know," he said hoarsely. "I need you, Haley. I was miserable being so far away from you, and from Eli. I love you—both of you. And I don't want to live my life without you. So I'm asking you to forgive me."

Not what she expected. "Forgive you?"

"For walking away. For leaving when I should have stayed. I can promise you that will never happen again. I won't leave you." He moved his hand to the back of her neck, leaning until his mouth hovered above hers. "I won't let you down. So will you—forgive me?"

"I already have."

His mouth claimed hers and Haley lost herself in the wonder of the man she loved…and the man who also loved her.

The kiss went on, and on, and on, until, weak-kneed, she collapsed against him.

He looked into her eyes and grinned. "Haley Calhoun," he said, "I'll do my very best…to make your every dream come true."

She kissed him again, relishing the feeling that she'd be kissing him, loving him, from this moment on. "You already have."

# Epilogue

"The women at the Cut and Curl outdid themselves," Haley said to the man at her side.

Her father laughed softly, patted her arm. "From what I've been told, they've been planning your wedding for years. They simply needed to figure out who the man would be. And I think they were tickled with the fact that you planned it for Valentine's Day. Gave them plenty to work with."

"Seemed perfect, especially since it's Gavin's birthday. I'd have never imagined my barn being transformed like this," she said, taking in the strings of lights that formed an illuminated ceiling and emphasized the mass of people on both sides of the aisle ahead. From all appearances, the entire town of Claremont and every child from Willow's Haven was in attendance.

"Oh, Theodore, she's gorgeous!" a woman's voice echoed through the crowd.

Haley recognized the voice immediately, because she heard it often, almost daily now, on the phone.

"Ivalene," her grandfather grumbled, "if you can't talk quiet, I'm going to make you go sit in the car." This was followed by a hefty "Oomph" as Ivalene elbowed him in the side. Which was followed by her grandfather's chuckle.

"I'm guessing they'll be the next ones down the aisle," her father said.

Which caused Haley to chuckle.

"Am I supposed to go now, Miss Haley?" Eli asked. He stood a few feet ahead of them, wearing a dashing black suit and a bow tie that his new daddy had helped him pick out and apparently tied "just right" earlier. The bright red bow tie matched the roses in her bouquet and went along with the theme for the day.

"Sure, you can," she said, smiling at the boy who, very soon, would carry a new last name.

The same one she'd have before this evening ended. She couldn't wait.

Holding a white pillow with the wedding bands tied to the top, Eli took a step forward but then stopped and turned around. "Wait," he said, and walked back to her.

A small tinge of panic shimmied down Haley's spine. Was he not happy about this? "Eli, what's wrong, honey?"

"I need to ask you a question."

She crouched to eye level with the little boy she adored. "Anything," she said. "What do you need to know?"

"Can I—" he slid his mouth to the side "—call you Mommy now?"

Her heart lodged in her throat, emotions beyond what she thought possible washing over her, filling her to the absolute brink…with joy. Love. Happiness.

"Oh, yes," she whispered. "I would like that very much."

He hugged her, and she heard the pillow hit the ground, but neither of them cared. "I love you, Mommy."

"I love you, too," she said, while her father, wiping away tears, picked up the pillow and handed it to his grandson.

"Okay, now," he said, clearing his throat. "I think this wedding is ready for us to get started. You ready, Eli?"

"Yes, sir!" he said.

He turned and started down the aisle, walking way faster than he'd been shown in the rehearsal, but earning an abundance of smiles, laughs and chuckles with every quick step.

Haley glanced forward and saw several of Eli's friends waving from their pews. Ben, of course, stood out, as he stepped into the aisle and grinned.

"When will you tell Ben?" her dad quietly asked.

She smiled. "We wanted to make sure everything was approved by the court, and that should happen next week, so it should be soon."

"I think it's great that Eli is going to have a brother so quickly."

She nodded. "And we can't wait to have both of them." Then she winked. "And maybe a few more eventually."

"Sounds great to me."

By the time Eli reached the front, he was practically skipping, and Haley laughed at his joy.

Then it was her turn.

The crowd stood and she saw her mother peeking down the aisle to get a glimpse.

And then she saw the man who, with each day, filled every part of her heart.

"Mr. Gavin!" Eli yelled, and the guests turned from viewing Haley to see about the commotion up front.

Haley stopped walking, curious to see what was about to happen between the two "men" of her family.

"That's Mommy. I can call her Mommy now," he said, loud enough for everyone to hear.

Haley saw several hands move to their mouths. But his next question was what brought them all to tears.

"Can I call you Daddy now, too?"

Gavin didn't miss a beat. He picked him up and swung him around. "I can't think of anything I'd like more."

"Except marrying Mommy?"

Gavin put their son on the ground, then looked down the aisle…and reached her heart.

"Except marrying Mommy," he agreed gruffly, then added, "my very best friend. And the woman I'll love always, till death do us part."

"Till death do us part," she whispered then glanced at her father and smiled.

"You ready?" he asked.

She looked down the aisle, toward the life full of dreams coming true that would start…right now.

*Thank You, God.*

"I'm ready."

\* \* \* \* \*

*Pick up these previous books in Renee Andrews's*
WILLOW'S HAVEN *series:*

*FAMILY WANTED*
*SECOND CHANCE FATHER*
*CHILD WANTED*

*Available now from Love Inspired!*

*Find more great reads at www.LoveInspired.com*

Dear Reader,

I've wanted to write Haley's story for quite some time, from the moment she was introduced in *Bride Wanted* and again in *Yuletide Twins*. She was the classic "always a bridesmaid, never a bride." I hope you enjoyed seeing her dream finally come true.

My goal for this story was to portray how much we need God in all of life's circumstances, not only when people exceed our expectations, but also when they let us down. Haley had been hurt in the past. Gavin, too, losing everything he cared about in the span of a few hours. But life often disappoints. God never does.

As always, I welcome prayer requests from my readers. Write to me at Renee Andrews, P.O. Box 8, Gadsden, AL, 35902 or through my email at renee@reneeandrews.com and I will gladly lift your requests to our Heavenly Father in prayer.

If you would like to keep up with me, my family, my books and my devotions online, please sign up for my newsletter and join my Facebook page: www.Facebook.com/AuthorReneeAndrews.

Blessings in Christ,
*Renee*

# COMING NEXT MONTH FROM
## Love Inspired®

### Available March 20, 2018

## THEIR AMISH REUNION
*Amish Seasons* • by Lenora Worth

Twelve years ago, Jeremiah Weaver left his Amish community—and the woman he loved—to join the Navy SEALS. Now he's back and determined to find his place among the Amish once again—and win the heart of the now-widowed Ava Jane...if she'll forgive him.

## ANNA'S FORGOTTEN FIANCÉ
*Amish Country Courtships* • by Carrie Lighte

Living with amnesia after a head injury, Anna Weaver must relearn why she fell for the fiancé she doesn't remember! Concerned Anna was planning to cancel their wedding before her accident, Fletcher Chupp is torn—should he reveal his fears and risk losing the woman he loves?

## COUNTING ON THE COWBOY
*Texas Cowboys* • by Shannon Taylor Vannatter

Cowboy Brock McBride signed up to build cabins at his friend's dude ranch—not to work with spirited event planner Devree Malone, who's helping decorate the structures. Yet the sparks between them are undeniable, and soon the tried-and-true country boy can't picture a life without the pretty city girl.

## THE BACHELOR'S PERFECT MATCH
*Castle Falls* • by Kathryn Springer

After agreeing to help Aiden Kane find his long-lost sister, librarian Maddie Montgomery is surprised at her instant attraction to the daredevil. As they uncover the truth, Aiden pushes Maddie out of her comfort zone—but he never imagined that in solving the puzzle of his past, he'd find the only woman he can imagine a future with.

## MOUNTAIN COUNTRY COURTSHIP
*Hearts of Hunter Ridge* • by Glynna Kaye

Lillian Keene moves to Hunter's Ridge to help her ill great-aunt keep her job at the Pinewood Inn. Denny Hunter has been sent from the big city to evaluate the establishment's worth—putting the two at odds. Can the businessman find common ground—and his happily-ever-after—with the small-town girl?

## REUNITED BY A SECRET CHILD
*Men of Wildfire* • by Leigh Bale

After the loss of his hotshot crew, Reese Hartnett returns to his hometown to heal—but it's shock he experiences when he learns he has a daughter! Katie Ashmore was heartbroken when Reese left her without a word, but watching Reese bond with their little girl, she wonders if there's hope for them to finally be a family.

---

**LOOK FOR THESE AND OTHER LOVE INSPIRED BOOKS WHEREVER BOOKS ARE SOLD, INCLUDING MOST BOOKSTORES, SUPERMARKETS, DISCOUNT STORES AND DRUGSTORES.**

LICNM0318

# Get 2 Free Books,
## Plus 2 Free Gifts—
### just for trying the Reader Service!

Love Inspired®

# SPECIAL EXCERPT FROM

*Love Inspired*®

*Ten years ago, Jeremiah Weaver left his Amish
community to become a navy SEAL. Now that he's back,
can he convince the woman he left behind—widow and
mother of two Ava Jane Graber—that he's here to stay?*

Read on for a sneak preview of
**THEIR AMISH REUNION**,
by **Lenora Worth**,
*available April 2018 from Love Inspired!*

"What are you doing here, Jeremiah?"

"I didn't want you to see me yet," he tried to explain.

"Too late." She adjusted her *kapp* with shaking hands.
"I need to go."

"Please, don't," he said. "I'm not going to bother you.
I…I saw you and I didn't have time to—"

"To leave again?" she asked, her tone full of more venom
than he could ever imagine coming from such a sweet soul.

"I'm not leaving," he said. "I've come back to Campton
Creek to help my family. But I had planned on coming to pay
you and Jacob a visit, to let you know that…I understand
how things are. You're married—"

"I'm a widow now," she blurted, two bright spots
forming on her cheeks. "I have to get my children home."

Kneeling, she tried to pick up her groceries, but his
hand on her arm stopped her. Jeremiah took the torn bag
and placed the thread, spices and canned goods inside the
bottom, the feel of sticky honey on his fingers merging with
the memory of her dainty arm. But the shock of her words

made him numb with regret.

*I'm a widow now.*

"I'm sorry," Jeremiah said in a whisper. "Beth never told me."

"You couldn't be reached."

Ah, so Beth had tried but he'd been on a mission.

"I wish I'd known. I'm so sorry."

Ava Jane kept her eyes downcast while she tried to gather the rest of her groceries and toss them into the torn bag.

"Here you go," he said, while her news echoed through his mind. "I'll go inside and get something to clean the honey."

Their eyes met as his hand brushed over hers.

A rush of deep longing shot through her eyes, jagged and fractured, and hit Jeremiah straight in his heart.

Ava Jane recoiled and stood. *"Denke."*

Then she turned and hurried toward the buggy. Just before she got inside, she pivoted back to give him one last glaring appraisal. "I wonder why you came back at all."

He watched as she got into the buggy and sat for a moment. Without a backward glance, Ava Jane held her head high. Then Jeremiah asked for a wet mop to clean the stains from the sidewalk. He only wished he could clean away the stains inside of his heart.

And just like her, he wondered why he'd returned to Campton Creek.

*Don't miss*
*THEIR AMISH REUNION by Lenora Worth,*
*available April 2018 wherever*
*Love Inspired® books and ebooks are sold.*

www.LoveInspired.com